ANOTHER HIDDEN SECRET

UMAR QUADEER

ANOTHER HIDDEN SECRETS

MERCILESS

ANOTHER HIDDEN SECRET

Mystery, Thriller & Suspense

UMAR QUADEER

Copyright © 2017, 2025 by Umar Quadeer. All rights reserved.

This is an upgraded and revised edition, released April 2025.
No part of this book may be used or reproduced in any form whatsoever without written permission except in the case of brief

quotations used in critical articles or reviews.

This book is a work of fiction. Names, characters, businesses, organizations, places, events, and incidents are either products of the imagination or are used fictitiously.
Any resemblance to actual persons, living or dead, events, or locales is entirely coincidental.

Printed in the United States of America.

For more information, or to book an event, contact:

merciless183@gmail.com

First Edition: August 2017
Upgraded Edition: April 2025

UMAR QUADEER

THINGS WILL NEVER BE THE SAME

A PAGE-TURNER BY UMAR QUADEER

PREVIOUSLY ON HER HIDDEN SECRETS

Bagz screamed to wakeup from a terrifying nightmare. He was gasping for air. He went to his dresser, looked at the obituary for Donna, and counted 20 missed calls from Ecstasy. "Another Day." He worried about the trouble that waiting in the darkness.

20

1 Year Later.

Reverend Don Franklin wiped the sweat from his forehead and took deep breaths. He looked to the side of him as his wife Riana lay fast asleep, he rose to his feet and walked into the bathroom. Turning on the faucet and feeling the cold water flowing on his palms. He then splashed the water on his face.

Don's condo was in darkness.

The only light that shined was the light in the bathroom.

He looked in the mirror and saw a dark figure behind him. It made his heart skip a beat. He gave a second look. "Hey!" He saw a masked figure standing at his back. He turned around immediately, and no one was in sight. *Too much whine.*

He shook his head and splashed more water on his face. He sighed and walked back to his bedroom. He pulled the blankets off his wife named Riana as he lay down. "Oh MY GOD," he said, jumping out of bed.

He ran towards the light switch. The bright light

shined across a sharp knife hanging out of Riana's bloody body. "OH! Lord," he yelled.

Behind him, the killer stood holding a Glock.

The reverend felt a sharp bullet entering his back and he struggled for his life, pushing the shooter up against the wall.

Don swung a hard punch trying to knock the killer to his knees but missed. He limped to the dresser for his gun until the pain slowed his movement. He felt a bullet enter the back of his head. "Ahh!" Don was hit with another fierce shot. The hot slug made its way out of Don's eye socket. The killer watched Don greet death.

ANOTHER HIDDEN SECRET was written in blood on the bedroom wall.

◆ ◆ ◆

"Happy birthday Grandma!" Ecstasy danced around the room, smiling with excitement.

"You shouldn't have," said Grandma Helen.

She and her grandma celebrated in her grandmother's room, making a nice memory.

Ecstasy smiled saying, "Birthday girl." Love, laughter, and fresh birthday cake filled the air.

Ecstasy carefully placed the birthday cake on a small, colorfully decorated table. "This is for the best grandma in the world."

"It smells wonderful." Grandma Helen blushed. The cake was decorated with beautiful icing and candles that glowed with a pleasant glow.

"Thank you, grandchild."

Ecstasy and her grandmother hugged and shared the moment as the music played. While dancing, their laughter filled the room.

"How old are you?" As they swirled and whirled, celebrating life and their special bond.

"I'm seventy-five." Ecstasy was grateful for her granny.

She treasured their time together, remembering her grandmother's knowledge and love.

"I wish Wolf could be here," said Ecstasy remembering her younger brother.

"We're gonna find him. don't worry." Grandma Helen meant every word. This birthday party showed their unbreakable relationship and joy in each other.

◆ ◆ ◆

Bagz sat at the bar with his two best friends, Nate and Tone. He took a sip of his beer and let out a heavy sigh.

"Man, I don't know what to do about Ecstasy," he shook his head.

"What's going on with you two?" Nate asked.

Bagz had another beer before responding.

"We're having major issues. Shit, I can't even explain."

Tone asked, "Man that girl is Coo-Coo if you ask me. She says she lives there with her grandmom. I never see anyone come out of that house but her."

Bagz glared at Tone. "Hell, yea."

Nate said, "Well, you do have a bit of a reputation for attracting some crazy hoes, Bagz."

Bagz smiled. "And with everything going on with Ecstasy, it's been even harder to deal with."

Tone touched Bagz's shoulder. "We're here for you, player, as needed,"

Bagz smirks. "Thanks, folks. Much appreciated."

They continued sitting at the bar, talking and drinking, trying to forget their problems for a little while. But Bagz knew that his problems would still be waiting for him when he left the bar.

They watched the basketball game until breaking news took over the TV. The newsroom was busy as Jessica prepared to report the newest breaking news. As she commented, her heart sank.

"Good evening. Sad news. Reverend Don Franklin and his wife Riana Franklin were murdered in their house.

Their remains were discovered early this morning by a neighbor who got concerned after noting their front door was left open."

Jessica took a deep breath before continuing, "The couple's deaths have been linked to the notorious Midnight Slasher. Like previous victims, 'Midnight' was written in blood on their bedroom wall."

The news crew looked horrified as she spoke. Fear and anxiety gripped the town.

The Franklin family has been a pillar of our community for many years," Jessica remarked. "Reverend Franklin was a beloved pastor, and his wife was a dedicated volunteer at the local homeless shelter. We sympathize with their family and friends."

The newscaster inhaled before continuing. "Anyone with knowledge about this crime or suspicious activities should contact police. We must work together to find this killer and stop this nightmare."

Jessica hoped the community would unite to stop the Midnight Slasher.

◆ ◆ ◆

Bagz parked his car in the small alley next to his apartment building. The poorly lit street lamps made long shadows on the ground, giving the place an eerie feel. After a long day, he just wanted to relax at home.

As he went up the creaky stairs to his apartment, Bagz felt a sense of mystery wash over him. When he opened the door, The smell of his favorite incense was still in the air, making the room feel calm.

Bagz was so tired that he couldn't wait to fall asleep on his bed. But he couldn't believe what he saw when he opened the bedroom door, he couldn't believe what he saw.

"OH. What the hell are you doing in my bed?" Bagz yelled, sounding both surprised and amused. He couldn't help but laugh at how bold she was.

Ecstasy slowly lifted her head, and her eyes sparkled with innocence. She gave Bagz a blank look as if to say, "What's wrong? "

Bagz crossed his arms and shook his head in shock. "Even better, how did you get into my apartment? Did you learn how to pick a lock or something?"

Ecstasy let out a soft meow as if Bagz's questions didn't worry her.

Ecstasy spread her legs, "You don't miss me, Daddy?"

Bagz didn't think it was a joke. "I'm not playing with you. You can't be popping up like this."

Ecstasy started to seduce Bagz acting like his sex slave.

"All right, fine," said Bagz, a smile pulling at the edges of her lips. "But next time, tell me before you come into my space, okay?"

Ecstasy reacted with a quiet mew as if to pledge her cooperation, but Bagz knew his feline companion was more than meets the eye.

Ecstasy gave him pleasure. With a shake of his head, Bagz moved to his side of the bed, moving Ecstasy's small body to the side. She reluctantly allowed him to lie down near her.

As Bagz fell into his soft bed, they started making love to one another again. It was something about how she moaned that made Bagz fall deeper into lust with her and how he held her tight that made Ecstasy feel like a little girl in his arms.

Soon after, Ecstasy began to pay attention as Bagz slept loudly. She thought he sounded cute, but another sound attracted her attention. The sound of missed calls and text messages turned her mood. She took a peek at the numerous woman and inappropriate texts that flashed across his screen, Ecstasy grew angry and closed her eyes to sleep.

Bagz woke up in the morning to an empty bed. "Where on earth is she?" He jumped out of bed and stumbled upon a note that was lying on the kitchen table.

Dear Bagz, you lying scumbag, you lowdown dirty scumbag, double-crosser! I should not have wasted my time trying to sort things out with you. I'm going to move on. Don't ever call me again. I mean it this time.

The next day, Ecstasy paced outside Pebbles' house, thinking about Bagz and their rocky relationship. She knew she needed to talk to someone, and Pebbles had always been a good listener. As she approached the front door, she noticed it was slightly ajar. *That's odd*, she thought. *Pebbles never leaves her door unlocked.* She hesitated before pushing the door open and calling her friend. "Hey girl, I'm coming upstairs! It's me Ecstasy!"

When she entered, "What the?"

Ecstasy was peeking out her bedroom window at Carlos.

"This mother fucker is suspect. I don't care what nobody says," said Pebbles.

She continued to spy on Carlos like the eyes of a pair of binoculars.

"What are you looking at?" Ecstasy inquired anxiously.

"For the last week you have been chasing this man around like a wild stalker, I mean look at you," she said, noticing the difference. "You're not yourself," said Ecstasy trying to talk some sense in Pebbles.

"Look, he has been dragging suspicious bags in his house. I saw him carrying a bag, and the bag dropped and guess what fell out the bag Ecstasy?"

"What fell out of the bag, Pebbles?"

"I don't trust that motherfucker."

Ecstasy cracked up. Pebbles looked into Ecstasy's eyes and saw that something wasn't right. "What's going on with you?"

Ecstasy thought about the night she spent with Bagz. And how she felt like she'd lost her best friend. "Bagz and I finally broke up."

"Again?"

"Yeah, he'll never change," she said.

"I could have told you about that."

Ecstasy's memory flashed, and thoughts of Bagz entered her mind.

"Right now, he's renting too much space in my head."

Ecstasy went toward the door.

"What about Cali? Why do you still worry about Bagz?" Pebbles said, following Ecstasy walking to the front door.

"Cali is a good man, and he treats me like a queen. But Bagz, he hit different."

Pebbles watched as Ecstasy left her home. She saw Ecstasy cross the street to get to her house. Pebbles felt that way again when she looked up at Ecstasy's window and saw that the blinds were moving. Pebbles closed the front door.

21

INVESTIGATION

The dimly lit strip club buzzed with energy as Bagz, Tone, and Nate found themselves immersed in the vibrant atmosphere. The air was filled with the throbbing rhythms of music, merging with the seductive dancing steps of the female performers on stage.

As they settled into a booth at the corner of the club, Bagz's mind was consumed by thoughts of Ecstasy. "I just can't be with only one," said Bagz, turning to Tone and Nate, he knew he needed their guidance and support.

Bagz leaned in, his voice barely heard over the club's vibrant atmosphere as the music pounded in the background. "I can't get Ecstasy out of my mind, man," he confessed, his eyes filled with a mix of determination and vulnerability. "I can't let her slip away that easy."

Tone, who is always the voice of reason, took a big breath and thought over Bagz's remarks. "Bro, we can't live with them and we can't live without them," he said, his tone laced with caution. "Let's stay getting this money."

Nate, the trio's free-spirited member, chimed in with a sly grin. "Let's toast to that."

Bagz sat back in his chair and thought about what they had said. He had a solid understanding that getting Ecstasy back wouldn't be simple. Her heart had been wounded, and her trust had been shattered.

Bagz said, "I hear you, man," his voice was full of resolve. "How can I convince her that I've changed, though?"

Nate chimed in; his eyes gleaming with mischief. "And remember, my man, timing is everything," he said, his voice filled with a hint of wisdom.

As the night at the club drew to a close, Bagz, Tone, and Nate left with a renewed sense of purpose. As they stepped out into the night, "I holla at yawl tomorrow." Bagz got in his car and drove away.

❖ ❖ ❖

Detective Carves and Roberts were sitting in the cramped, cluttered office of the forensics lab, anxiously waiting for the results of the DNA testing. The cellar where the missing woman was located yielded hair and urine samples.

The technician entered with a heavy file.

"Detectives," she said, "I have the results of the DNA testing from the cellar."

Carves and Roberts leaned forward, watching the

technician. The technician flipped over the file and remarked, "The cellar DNA samples match Carlos' Bundy DNA profile."

Carves and Roberts looked incredulous. "Carlos?" Carves repeated to comprehend.

"Yes," the tech said. "We ran a comparison with the DNA on file from the Jeffrey Dahmer poster that was found in the cellar, and it was a match."

Roberts scoffed. "I can't believe it," he whispered.

Carves nodded. "We need to get a warrant for his arrest," he stood up. "We can't let him get away with this."

As they made their way out of the lab, Carves and Roberts couldn't help but feel a sense of relief that they finally had a lead in the case.

Carlos Bundy paced back and forth in his living room. "What are the police doing here?" He was a nervous wreck as he looked through his blinds. "Oh Lord," he said to himself as the loud banging on the door demanded his attention.

"Anybody home?" Detective Carves stood with his hand close to his gun and his partner backing his every move.

"Who is it?" Carlos asked with a kind voice.

"It's the police. You mind opening?"

The sound of the door unlocking caught the Detective's attention as they prepared for the worse.

The door slowly opened. "Yes, what can I do for you officers?" asked Carlos.

"You mind if we come inside for a minute?" Carves asked.

"Sure, come on in," said Carlos pretending not to be nervous.

Carves and Roberts stepped inside with their eyes darting around and at everything in sight. They noticed an old beer bottle on the wooden kitchen table. They gazed at each other.

"Do me a favor and put your hands behind your back, Carlos."

Carlos screamed. "No, hell no, you will never catch me alive!" and charged at Detective Carves.

Carves picked up Carlos and slammed him.

Carlos hit the ground hard. Carlos reached for the gun. Carves pulled his arm. They both wrestled for possession of the handgun.

"Freeze Carlos! Freeze!" said Roberts aiming his gun at them and trying to get a clear shot at Carlos.

Carlos elbowed Carves in the ribs. He reached for the gun.

"Freeze motherfucker, or I will shoot," said Roberts.

"We need backup on 1224 Parish Street." Carves stuck his knee into Carlos's back and handcuffed him.

"You tried to take my gun?" He kicked Carlos in the ribs three times.

"That's enough, Carves," said Roberts shoving him away from Carlos.

"Let's not forget about why we are here," said Roberts.

The Takedown and Arrest of Carlos Bundy

The city buzzed with anticipation as the evening news

began to unfold, and the anchor's voice boomed through living rooms across the region. The television flashed to life, depicting the common scene from a news studio, and the headline at the bottom of the screen read: "Detectives Carves and Roberts Arrest Dangerous Female Trafficker Carlos Bundy."

In the newsroom, reporters frantically shuffled papers and adjusted their microphones, anxious to report the most recent breaking news. Jennifer Evans, the main reporter, stood poised in front of the camera, her face showing a mix of seriousness and enthusiasm as she prepared to share the contents of the investigation that had gripped the city for months.

"Good evening, viewers. We have breaking news about the investigation into a known human trafficking ring," Jennifer said in a voice that got everyone's attention. "Detectives Antonio Carves and Michael Roberts have made a significant breakthrough in their relentless pursuit of justice,"

The video then transitioned to a scene from a news conference, in which Detectives Carves and Roberts were shown standing next to one another while displaying determined attitudes. Banners behind them read "Together for a Safer Community" and included the department's logo.

Jennifer continued, her voice filled with admiration, "These two dedicated detectives, working tirelessly day and night, managed to apprehend the notorious trafficker known as Carlos Bundy. Today, Bundy was taken into custody, and after being interrogated, he admitted his responsibility for these horrible offenses.

The video then cut to a picture of Carlos Bundy, a

threatening-looking man whose icy stare sent shivers down the spines of those who were watching it. Jennifer's voice intensified as she shared the shocking details that had come to light during the investigation.

"Carlos Bundy, a notorious figure, has successfully eluded capture for a significant amount of time. He was the one who was responsible for trafficking vulnerable women over state boundaries, putting them through unspeakable traumas in the process. But because of Detectives Carves and Roberts' tireless persistence and unflinching dedication, his reign of terror has finally come to an end."

Jennifer's tone was filled with pleasure as she continued, saying, "In recognition of their exceptional service and their significant contribution to safeguarding our community, the police department has awarded both Detective Carves and Detective Roberts a promotion that is well-deserved." They have shown extraordinary bravery and unflinching dedication, going above and above to protect the safety of our citizens.

On the screen appeared now the amazed expressions of Detective Carves and Detective Roberts as they shook hands with the Chief of Police, who sported a pleased grin on his face.

22

New Beginning

Ecstasy sat at her vanity, staring at her reflection in the mirror. Her heart fluttered with nervous excitement as she held her phone tightly in her hand. Cali's name illuminated the screen, and she knew it was the call she had been waiting for.

Taking a deep breath, Ecstasy answered the call, her voice filled with anticipation. "Hey, Cali. I've been looking forward to this."

Cali's voice came through the phone, warm and comforting. "Hey, Ecstasy. Me too. I thought we could go to this new Italian restaurant downtown. What do you think?"

Ecstasy smiled. "That sounds perfect, Cali. I'll meet you there at 7."

Hanging up the phone, Ecstasy felt a rush of excitement and nerves wash over her. This was her chance to move on from Bagz, the guy who had hurt her so deeply. But the anguish caused by their breakup continued to linger, and she needed some guidance to help her open her heart again.

Just as she was lost in her thoughts, her grandmother Helen entered the room. Helen was a wise and loving woman, who had always been there for Ecstasy through thick and thin. She had seen Ecstasy go through heartbreak before and knew just what to say to help her granddaughter find her inner strength.

Helen sat down next to Ecstasy and placed a gentle hand on her shoulder. "My dear, remember, love is a journey, and sometimes we encounter detours along the way. Bagz was one of those detours, but now it's time for you to move forward."

Ecstasy nodded, tears welling up in her eyes. "I know, Grandma. It's just hard sometimes. Bagz hurt me so much."

Helen wiped away a tear from Ecstasy's cheek. "I understand, my sweet girl. But you are strong, and you deserve someone who will treat you with kindness and respect. Cali could be that person, but you have to be willing to let go of the pain and embrace the possibilities of a new beginning."

Ecstasy took a deep breath, absorbing her grandmother's words of wisdom. She realized that she couldn't let the past define her future. Cali was offering her a chance at happiness, and she couldn't let fear hold her back.

With newfound determination, Ecstasy stood up and walked over to her closet. She carefully selected a vibrant, knee-length red dress, symbolizing her readiness to embrace passion and love again. She paired it with her favorite pair of black heels, feeling empowered with every step she took.

As she stood in front of the mirror, she felt her

grandmother's presence behind her, guiding her through the transformation. Helen smiled approvingly, her eyes filled with love and pride. "You look stunning, my dear. Now go out there and let your light shine."

Ecstasy took one final look at herself, feeling a surge of confidence and hope. She grabbed her purse and headed towards the door, ready to embark on a new chapter of her life.

With her grandmother's words echoing in her mind, Ecstasy knew that she was not just getting ready for a date. She was getting ready to let go of the past, to embrace the present, and to open her heart to a future filled with love and happiness.

Ecstasy sat on the couch in her living room. "Cali should arrive any second now. Her mind started to reflect on her childhood bedroom.

The room was dimly lit, with tattered curtains barely covering the small window. Ecstasy was seated on the old carpet with her back against the wall. She could hear her brother sobbing because he was being hurt. He stormed into the room after his beating. Then he walks in and sits down next to her. Wolf, who is scared and determined at the same time, looks at her.

"Wolf, I've had enough," Ecstasy said in a whisper. "We need to figure out how to get out of here."

Wolf begins nodding, "Let's do it tonight, Ecstasy. This cruel way of life isn't good enough for us. We need to leave."

They saw each other. They both knew that the way to freedom was at Grandma Helen's house. She always had their back through hard times. They were both determined to get there, which gave them confidence.

Ecstasy said with tears in her eyes, "Remember when Mom used to be kind?"

Wolf squeezed her hand, "Ecstasy, I miss them days. But now that things have changed, we can't live this way anymore. We have to watch out for each other."

She thinks about how she and Wolf would put their most valuable things in a small bag. They give each other a knowing look, and their hearts start to beat faster.

When the coast was clear they headed out the door and didn't look back. Ecstasy and Wolf walked together down a noisy street full of gangs. The warm rays of the sun kiss their faces, giving them hope and a sense of freedom.

Ecstasy starts to smile and asks Wolf, "Can you imagine? No more worries. "No more pain."

"We'll find Grandma's house," says Wolf, grinning.

The real-world crashes in and breaks up her daydream from the loud sound of her phone ringing. Cali was calling Ecstasy on the phone.

Ecstasy fights back tears, her heart pounding with the burden of her memories. At last, she picked up the phone.

"Hey, baby." She smiled.

"I'm outside." He double-parked.

"Ok, I'm leaving now." She headed out the door.

Bagz and Tone stalked Ecstasy from across the street. "There goes your girl." Tone pointed at Ecstasy.

"Man, she's not mine," Bagz said and watched Ecstasy get

into Cali's double-parked Jaguar.

Ecstasy and Cali drove up the road, Bagz was envious.

That night, Ecstasy sat across from Cali at a candlelit table in a fancy restaurant, a radiant smile gracing her face.

"Thank you so much for the flowers," Ecstasy got seated.

"I never experienced anything like this."

"Like what?"

"You showered me with love, attention, and plenty of gifts."

The waiter bought their plates out.

"Thank you."

As they ate each bite of their delicious meal, Ecstasy couldn't help but feel a sense of joy and contentment.

"You always doing nice things for me."

"I'm really into you Ecstasy. I spent the time carefully preparing the evening, making sure every part was perfect. From the bouquet of your favorite flowers to the exquisite jewelry that decorated your wrist, it's clear that I had put a lot of thought into making you feel cherished."

"I could do this forever," she smiled. "We have a lot of common interests."

"Our conversations flow easily."

"I feel a deep connection forming—a bond that outdid the phony. " She looked at the missed calls from Bagz on her phone. "I'm amazed at how you seemed to anticipate my every need, being with you gives me the feeling of comfort and security."

Cali leaned across the table as the evening came to an end and took Ecstasy's hand in his. His eyes sparkled with affection as he expressed his admiration for her. "Girl, you look so sexy." Ecstasy's heart pounded as he continued, "You looking better by the second."

"Let's go to your place." Ecstasy waited for a response.

"Okay, because it will serve as a haven where our bond could grow in the most personal of ways. You know what I mean?"

◆ ◆ ◆

The air was cool as they entered the room.

The room had a soft, dim light, casting a warm glow over their entwined bodies. "You feel so good baby," said Cali.

After kissing her in bed, they both got naked.

Their movements were slow and deliberate as if they were savoring every moment of this newfound intimacy.

"Don't stop," She made a sensuous moaning noise.

Ecstasy moaned loudly. As they lay together, their bodies intertwined, Ecstasy felt a profound sense of bliss and vulnerability. It was a moment of pure surrender—he left her breathless and filled with a sense of fulfillment she had never experienced before. "Cali! Cali!" she yelled full of passion.

Afterward, they lay side by side, their fingers tracing gentle patterns on each other's skin.

In the quiet stillness of the night, the buzzing of Ecstasy's phone stopped her from sleeping. She read her text messages. "You love him more than me? Are you happy now? Does he fuck you better than me? I loved Donna more than you anyway bitch. Fuck you," said Bagz.

Ecstasy got furious reading her text messages.

23

TRANSMISSION SLIPPING

Ecstasy sat on the sofa with mixed emotions. "I hate Bagz." She cried to Grandma Helen for comfort and advice.

"Who. What's wrong?"

Her voice shook as she talked, "My new boyfriend. He treated me well, but I couldn't get away from my past with Bagz."

"Calm down grandchild tell me all about it."

"He crushed my heart; he was a cheater and liar. I wake up crying every night, thinking about Bagz. I couldn't answer Cali's calls during my stress. My heart remained madly in love with a man who doesn't love me back." Grandma Helen listened attentively, her expression showing empathy and wisdom. She gently took Ecstasy's hand and spoke with expertise.

"Child, I can see the battle you're fighting within yourself," Grandma Helen said gently. "But sometimes we must step back to replenish our strength. Bagz had your heart, but he shouldn't rule your happiness."

Ecstasy's eyes lit up as Grandma Helen spoke with determination. "Let's try something else, darling. Get Bagz's social media photo. We'll release his hold on your heart."

"Okay, Grandma." Ecstasy followed her grandmother's advice.

"He's going to wish he was dead." She anxiously took Bagz's picture. Grandma Helen led Ecstasy through the ceremony with shaky hands as the candles filled the room.

The lights flickered and then went out. Ecstasy's heart raced in the darkness.

❖ ❖ ❖

Bagz took a deep breath, got out of the car, and walked up to Ecstasy's house. "Ecstasy?"

He began knocking, hoping Ecstasy would answer.

The house rang with a knock. Bagz's desire to re-enter Ecstasy's life was evident. She moved toward the entrance, a shine of hope rekindling within her.

Grandma Helen's warm but strong voice eased the strain. "Don't answer it, my dear," she murmured. "Bagz faces only the chaos. Karma will get him."

They sat in the dark, hands interlocked, while the knocks continued. The house quieted, and the flickering candles symbolized Ecstasy's inner light.

Ecstasy discovered her power in that instant. She realized her heart could heal, release Bagz's toxic grip, and embrace a brighter future.

◆ ◆ ◆

Bagz knocked a couple more times. *No answer?* "Man, fuck this shit," he said and headed down the stairs with a slight headache.

Suddenly, without warning, two black SUVs swerved in front of him screeching tires! Gangsters jumped out with guns drawn. "Get the fuck down now!" they screamed. "Aw, shit!" Bagz said, holding his hands up. "Don't shoot."

The gunmen escorted Bagz to the SUV by gunpoint. Bagz had thoughts of going to jail until he saw Spank sitting in the front seat. "Fuck!" he said, as he was being pushed into the back seat of the tinted SUV.

"What's up Bagz?" Spank asked, sitting comfortably in the backseat. His goons checked Bagz's pockets and waist for guns, cash, and house keys.

"What are you out of your fucking mind?"

"I told you to stop playing with me, didn't I?" said Spank, pushing a stun gun to Bagz's chest knocking him unconscious.

◆ ◆ ◆

Tone gasped when he watched Bagz, his best friend, forced into a van by a gang of threatening figures.

Tone immediately stood up, knocking down a lamp. He ran out the door with his handgun.

As he ran outside and aimed at the fleeing SUV. He didn't want to hurt Bagz accidentally. "Bitch ass nigaz'." He struggled with the car keys, his pulse beating with terror and purpose as the engine started. "Regardless, I got to save Bagz."

Tone drove through the shadowy streets in his car, battling the night traffic.

The SUV transporting Bagz was a few vehicle lengths ahead, its red taillights flashing.

Tone gripped the steering wheel tighter. He followed the van's taillights, staying close but not too nearby. He didn't want Spank's crew to notice him.

He pondered. Tone knew he had to help his comrade despite the chaos.

Tone toughened as the chase continued through the winding streets. "Ima kill, them!" Adrenaline numbed his anxiety and mistrust.

With each turn and acceleration, he pushed himself to the limits, his mind focused on a single objective. "I got you, bro!"

A deserted storehouse stopped the Suvs.

◆ ◆ ◆

A loud smack to Bagz's face got his undivided attention. "Come on, man. What do yawl want?" said Bagz hanging upside down from a chain connected to the ceiling of an unknown location. His face was beaten and bloody. Spank and his crew surrounded Bagz. They all took a break from beating him.

"I'm going to ask you one more fucking time, where the stash at?" asked Spank, the room was full of gangsters.

"I told you, it's at my crib man, let me down." Bagz was in severe pain, swinging back and forth with blood rushing to his head.

"I have been told ya' bitch ass to get down with my squad, but you want to go and fuck with Stephon," said Spank as he kicked Bagz in the face.

"I'll get down with y'all niggas, man damn," said Bagz. His mind was on survival. *I'm not going to die. I'm not going to die*!

"It's too late now nigga, Stephon got a lot of enemies' Am I right Germane?" said Spank.

Germane emerged from a crowd of hoodlums; rage filled his heart. He approached Bagz.

"You had my bitch bagging up coke for you, nigga?" Germane punched Bagz so hard in the mouth, that it cut Germaine's knuckles.

Bagz spits a bloody tooth out on the floor. The pain was unbearable.

"That wasn't my fault," he said, barely managing his words.

"Chill, Germane let's get the money first, and then kill this nigga," said Spank.

He grabbed Germaine's hand. "You just going to have to put

your killing urge on hold.

He looked Bagz in his eyes. "Which one of these keys is the one to your house?" he asked.

"Were the safe at? And the combination to the safe. I know you got one." Bagz better start talking or he was dead.

"The silver one, with the black dot on it. The combination is 4567354. The safe is in my hallway closet," said Bagz.

Germane eyes glowed with anger thinking about Tosha. Her face kept flashing in his mind.

"What's Stephon's address?" Germane asked, walking closer to Bagz, who was still hanging upside down.

"I don't know." Bagz lied.

Germane stared at Bagz's hanging body and grabbed his cheek and squeezed his mouth open.

He placed a lit cigarette on Bagz's tongue.

Bagz screamed from the burning sensation on his lips and gums.

"What's the address?" Germane yelled and threw the cigarette in Bagz's mouth.

Bagz had enough. "Ok, I'll give it to you!" he said, spitting out the lit cigarette.

"3467 Harrison Lane."

"The shit better be there when I get there, or I'm going to torture you when I get back," said Spank.

Spank and his crew walked towards the door.

"Man, Man you stay outside the door and watch this bitch

until we get back."

"Bet. I got you."

◆ ◆ ◆

Tone cautiously entered the warehouse after taking a big breath. He proceeded silently, trying not to alert Spank and his crew.

Tone watched through a broken window, his heart sinking. Bagz was chained and terrified. Spank and his crew walked out of the room, his wicked laughter filling the enormous hall. The group made it to the parking lot. Spank jumped inside the SUVs and his crew drove away.

Tone's anger drove him. He had to act fast. With his gun raised, he prepared to enter the fight, bracing himself for the unknown dangers that lay ahead.

.

◆ ◆ ◆

Bagz was trying desperately to unchain himself, while Tone was on his way to rescue him. He watched upside down, the weak connection from the chain to the ceiling. He began to put pressure on the chain, trying to break it loose from the ceiling.

◆ ◆ ◆

On the other side of town Spank, Germane, and Donny were in Bagz's house as if they were in a toy store. They were shopping for every valuable they could get their hands on.

"Here go the safe!" Germane yelled, and then pulled

out a piece of paper, with the combination written on it.

Spank used the numbers then opened the safe and smiled. "The motherfucker wasn't lying after all," Spank said, as the gangsters began filling the bags up with money and drugs.

24

HATRED

"Wake up," said Stephon. Tosha tossed and turned until her puppy eyes opened.

"What is it, boo?" Tosha asked half-sleep.

"I'm hungry, can you fix me something to eat?"

"What do you want to eat boo?"

"One of their bacon and cheese egg sandwiches?"

"You are so greedy, I got to feed that belly." She kissed his stomach down to his dick.

"I'll deal with him when I get back," she said, grabbing her earbuds and heading out the bedroom door.

Tosha worked herself in the kitchen, the aroma of a delicious dinner filling the air. The sound of sizzling ingredients and the clatter of pots and pans were abruptly interrupted by the sharp chime of the doorbell.

She was startled, so she wiped her hands on her apron

before rushing to the front door.

"Just a minute," she said racing to the door.

"I have a package for Tosha Evens, that need needs your signature."

She noticed the man in a UPS uniform holding a package firmly in his hands as she peeked through the peephole. Relief washed over her; it was the package she had been eagerly waiting for. Excitement surged through Tosha as she swung the door open, a warm smile on her face.

She was initially happy, but as the door opened, she became unsure and afraid. The UPS driver wore an unsettling expression, his eyes filled with an intensity that sent a chill down Tosha's spine. Before she could react, her heart pounding in her chest, Donny swiftly pressed a cold, hard object against her chest.

Her eyes widened, and she felt her breath seize in her throat as if time had stopped. It wasn't the package she had expected; it was a gun.

Donny snarled; his voice filled with dread. "Don't make a sound," he commanded. "Let's enter silently."

Donny's grip on the gun remained firm as he guided Tosha further into the house, his intentions shrouded in mystery. Her thoughts raced, as they entered the living room, Donny's demeanor shifted. His eyes narrowed; his voice lowered to a menacing whisper.

He cursed, "Listen carefully, Tosha. I'm not here to take your life. But I will if I have to."

Then Germane and Spank walked inside the house. "Hey baby, you miss me?" said Germane.

"What the hell are you doing in my house?" She charged at Germane and yelled but Donny covered her mouth with his hand wrapped in a leather glove."

"Let me see that bitch," Germane took hold of her with a tight grip. "You thought you were gone' play me like this?"

Donny zip-tied her hands behind her back.

Spank said, "Where's Stephon?"

Germane put her in a headlock and then started choking her, "answer him."

"Upstairs in bed," she said catching her breath.

Germane held the gun tight to her head. He whispered. "You bet not say a word."

"Point to where the bed room at bitch," Germane was mad.

"Why are you doing this to me?" Tosha words were followed by tears.

He said in a low tone, "Bitch I'll kill you right now." The gun was pressed against her temple.

Stephon lay in the comfort of his bed, his mind drifting into dreams. But the peace was immediately broken by the piercing strike to his forehead.

"Wake the fuck up bitch!" said Donny.

Stephon's eyes shot open. Before he could comprehend what was happening, three masked figures appeared in the room, their presence heavy with menace.

Tosha cried. "I'm sorry Stephon, he made me?"

"Yo let her go!" Stephon's eyes widened as he realized the awful scenario scene unfolding before him. His girlfriend was held at gunpoint by Germane.

Donny, said in a firm, commanding voice, "Stay still, and don't make a sound. Cooperate, and no one gets hurt."

Stephon's thoughts were racing with questions and potential solutions. The intruders were after something specific, and it became apparent as their demands echoed through the room. They were after, "I want the money and the combination to the safe."

"Somebody set me up." Stephon's conscience was tormented by guilt.

"The safe is in that closet behind you. don't hurt her."

Stephon agreed, disclosing the location of the safe and the combination with caution and a sad heart. Fear mingled with anger as he watched the gunmen, manhandle his girlfriend.

"Jackpot." As the safe was opened, the intruders' anticipation grew, their greed obvious in the air. But Stephon was aware that the looted valuables were only temporary material goods that could be replaced. He would not allow Tosha to suffer since he valued her safety and well-being.

He lunged at Donny in a sudden surge of defiance.

Chaos erupted in the room as the struggle ensued.

Stephon fought bravely.

"I'll kill you." He reached for the gun as they tussled. Gunshots were echoing through the room.

Stephon's body slowly dropped to the carpet filling it with his blood."

"Stupid motherfucka." Donny was out of breath.

Tosha cried. She dropped to the ground-hugging on Stephon's dead body.

"What the fuck —!" said Germane, looking out the window for any witnesses.

"Let's get this money," said Spank noticing Stephon's dead body on the floor and Tosha weeping over him covered in blood.

"Just take the money and go," said Tosha.

"Man, fuck that, kill the bitch, and let's go," said Donny.

"My bitch wasn't supposed to die, my nigga."

Donny and Spank begin filling the bags up with everything in the safe.

Germane was in a rage, "This is the moment I have been waiting for Was it worth it?"

He smiled, then frowned. "Fuck you, bitch!" he said, then held a pillow over her face.

Tosha screamed. "Stop it!"

Germane began to smother Tosha. with the pillow. Tosha was in tears and out of breath, and her circulation was short, almost unconscious Tosha begins to fade into non-existence. On the verge of dying, she said, "God, please don't let me die."

"Tell the truth, I fucked you the best," he said with an insane star.

Donny aimed his gun at Tosha.

"Chill." Germane pushed Donny's arm. "She died."

"She, better be," said Donny.

After they robbed and killed Stephon and Tosha, the trio drove back to the warehouse. They sat in the tinted-out SUV riding the streets of Philly. They were wearing bullet-proof gear, and guns were ready to blast.

Spank parked, looked around as he sat inside, slumped down in the seat, and rolled a blunt. He lit up a joint and took in the view out the back window as he surveyed the parking lot. Alley cats jumped from rubbish piles.

Donny couldn't stop laughing.

Germane said, "What's so funny motherfucker?"

"Germane you crazy. She must of broke your heart the way you smothered your girl like that?"

"Watch what you say out ya mouth. Don't ever talk about that again," Germane said.

"Well, she better be dead because if she not'," said Donny.

"If she's not, what?" Germane asked.

Spank passed the blunt to Germane. "Chillout. We need to kill Bagz before all this shit hits the fan."

ANOTHER HIDDEN SECRETS

25

CREEPING WHILE YOU SLEEPING

Tone breathed and crept toward the entryway. He hid behind a cold brick wall as he approached. He saw only a single guard watching a security monitor as he turned around. Tone, couldn't miss his chance. He braced, carefully pressing his gun's trigger.

It was time. As the guard turned away from the monitor, Tone quickly raised his pistol and aimed it at the target. The warehouse echoed with the gunfire, and the guard collapsed.

Tone moved quickly after eliminating the threat. He ran and approached the door, his mind racing with expectation and horror. The door creaked open, revealing a dark area with a wet, depressing smell.

In the center of the room, Bagz dangled upside down from a rusting chain. Tone's heart tightened, boosting his drive.

"Bagz, it's me. I've come to get you out of here."

Relief and filled surprise-filled Bagz's gaze. "Tone? Is that you?"

Tone nodded, scanning the room for potential dangers. "It's me. We don't have much time. Can you hold on a little longer?"

Bagz smiled uncomfortably. "Tone, you know I'm tough. Just get me down from here."

Tone grabbed a container and dragged it under Bagz.

With a swift motion, he leaped onto the crate, balancing precariously as he cut through the chains with a small tool from his pocket. Bagz collapsed into Tone's arms when the metal links broke.

Bagz groaned as pain shot up through his body, but his appreciation shined brilliantly in his eyes. "Thank you, Tone. I knew I could depend on you."

Tone spoke with conviction. "We're not out of here yet, Bagz. We need to make it out of here, fast."

Helping Bagz, Tone directed him towards the exit, their movements smooth and deliberate. They walked through the warehouse's labyrinth, watchful for Spank and his gang.

Tone noticed movement near the exit. He leaned Bagz back into the shadows, his heart pounding. Spank and his henchman. Their words were laced with malice from beginning to end. "Bagz is probably still hanging around," said Donny. The violent laughter of the individuals could be heard bouncing off the warehouse's brick walls.

◆ ◆ ◆

Germane, Spank, and Donny made it inside the warehouse. Spank opened the door and walked inside, and froze, his mouth dropped, and he looked at Donny. Donny was instantly shocked. "This can't be happening." The chains lay on the ground, and Bagz was gone.

◆ ◆ ◆

Bagz lay in a hospital bed, his body battered and broken, with fractured ribs, and a broken jaw, bearing the physical remains of his recent ordeal.

As he fought through the haze of pain and confusion, two figures entered his room—Detectives Carves and Roberts.

Experienced and thorough detective Carves approached Bagz with caution. Detective Roberts, his colleague, stood calmly by his side as he looked around the room with a stern attitude. Carves cleared his throat and spoke in a soft but perceptive manner.

"Bagz, let's figure out what happened. Can you provide any information regarding the circumstances leading up to your injuries?"

Bagz's mind raced, torn between the fear of revenge and the weight of his conscience. His first inclination was to lie, to make up a story that would protect him and others he cared about. He hesitated for a moment, his eyes darting between the detectives, searching for a way out.

Bagz inhaled deeply. "I was carjacked and beat up and left to die on the side of the road." He spun a web of half-truths and false alibis, painting a picture that had entangled his life.

"I didn't see who it was they wore masks."

His words flowed with practiced ease, disguising the true extent of his involvement.

Detective Carves listened closely while looking past Bagz's mask. "I see."

"No. I don't know." A hint of mistrust could be seen in his eyes, suggesting that Bagz's comments may not be entirely truthful.

"Is that right?" Carves exchanged a knowing glance with Roberts, silently conveying their shared skepticism.

However, just as the detectives were about to make a move, their focus suddenly changed. News reached Carves police radio about a suspicious incident at Tosha's residence, she was fighting for her life, prompting swift police action.

Reports of suspicious men fleeing the scene led them to rush Tosha to the same hospital.

The arrival of Tosha, who was unconscious and frail, caused the investigation's focus to change. "What a busy night." Detectives Carves and Roberts rushed to her side, leaving Bagz momentarily forgotten.

As they delved into the details of the incident at Tosha's house, a chilling revelation emerged.

Bagz wondered what was going on feeling guilty he gave up Stephon's address to Spank to save his own life.

Bagz was overcome with fear as he thought about the image of his friend Tone, facing imprisonment for a crime he had committed, weighing heavily upon him. "Fuck!"

Detective Carves came back in the room, "I want to ask you about the Midnight slasher killing of your girlfriend Donna."

Upon hearing Donna's name, Bagz's heart began to race. Memories of her radiant smile and gentle nature flooded his mind, intermingling with the pain of her loss. He forced a hard swallow as he struggled to contain his agony.

Carves asks Bagz, "Just want to help get her justice," Detective Carves concentrated his penetrating eyes on Bagz.

"Mabey this slasher is after you."

The detectives spoke with a mixture of haste and interest to draw conclusions that would take them to the truth.

"Bagz, I want to know more details about Donna and her life. We're looking for any connections that could help us understand how she was killed."

"She did not deserve what happened to her."

Detective Roberts, standing nearby, interjected with a solemn nod. "Bagz, you're right. Nobody should suffer such a destiny. To get Donna justice, we're doing everything we can."

Detective Carves persisted in his line of inquiry, keeping an eye out for any scrap of knowledge that would help direct their inquiry.

Bagz's thoughts raced as he combed through Donna's

recollections for any indications of hostility or unsolved issues. The weight of guilt settled heavily upon him as he wracked his brain for answers. *Could I have missed something? Had I failed to keep her safe?*

"I... I can't think of anyone, Detective," Bagz replied, his voice tinged with a mix of frustration and sorrow.

"Donna had a heart of gold. She had no enemies. This is not what she deserved."

Detective Carves nodded, realizing how much anguish Bagz was going through. "We trust you, Bagz. These things are frequently more personal than we initially think. We'll keep digging, uncovering every lead, until we find the truth."

Unveiling the Faces

Tosha was lying in her hospital bed, her body still frail from the terrifying experience she had just gone through. Antiseptic fumes flooded the space, serving as a continual reminder of the struggle she had to wage to preserve her life. As she gazed out the window, lost in her thoughts, a knock on the door interrupted her reverie.

Detectives Carves and Roberts walked into the room with a look of resolve on their faces. They carried a folder containing surveillance footage and a series of photographs, and evidence gathered.

"Hello, Tosha. I'm back with some good news."

Carves approached her bed with a gentle smile, his eyes reflecting compassion and a burning desire to bring closure to her ordeal. "Just need your time."

Roberts stood close by, providing constant support.

"Tosha, we've made some progress in the investigation," Carves began, his voice filled with sincerity.

"We've obtained surveillance footage from the vicinity of your home on the day of the incident. With the help of our forensic team."

He handed Tosha the folder, and she cautiously opened it, her eyes scanning the images before her. The faces of three men stared back at her, their expressions captured in frozen moments. One face sprang up as being recognized, triggering a memory-deep spark of recognition. "Get them away from me."

Carves drew nearer and pointed at the first picture.

"This man here, we ran his prints and discovered he has an active warrant out for his arrest. He had a big part to play in what happened that night, in our opinion."

"That's him. The man who shot Stephon." Tosha nodded, her heart pounding in her chest. "I know their voices from hanging with Germane." The pieces were slowly coming together, and the path to justice was becoming clearer. Carves then went to the second image while still speaking firmly.

"This man has a criminal record, with a history of violence," he explained. "We think he may have helped attack your house. Can you place either of these people?"

Tosha's gaze fixed on the familiar face, her mind retracing the haunting memories of that fateful night.

Slowly, she nodded, "Yes. Him too," her voice filled with a mix of determination and relief.

Last but not least. She was upset looking at Germane's mug shot. "My X boyfriend," she said in rage. "That's them," her voice resonating with the force of her bravery. "I remember them. I can identify all of these men."

Carves and Roberts exchanged a glance, a glimmer of hope shining in their eyes.

◆ ◆ ◆

The next day A white Range Rover swerved in front of a crowded corner! Bagz jumped out, holding a fist full of cash! "Who wants to get paid?" Bagz's face was bruised, the overnight stay at the hospital had given him enough time to think of his next move. "This is ten racks! Who wants it?!"

"What the hell happened to you?" said Nate.

Bagz walked with aggression and spoke words of boiling rage. His face was swollen. "Who wants this money?" He asked with a fist full of cash. "Who wants it!? Who wants to put some work in?"

I got Geez for anybody that puts a bullet in Spank's fuckin' head; I want him dead!" he screamed.

◆ ◆ ◆

The next day "Ever since I met you, my life has been good," said Ecstasy. She enjoyed Cali's company. "I'm having the time of my life." Cali didn't respond. He was in a daze staring at the ceiling of his hotel room. Ecstasy sensed a problem, "may I ask what is wrong with you?"

"I'm good. What made you ask me that?" He didn't realize

how different he was acting.

"All day you haven't been your regular happy self."

"Okay, you got me I'm in a jam. I'm working on my new book, and I have writer's block. My publishers are breathing down my back. But nothing I seem to write is good enough."

Ecstasy thought hard, "I have a good story for you to write."

"I'm serious, and you are playing games," he said, shaking his head. He lit up a cigarette.

"I'm not playing, and it would be perfect."

"Okay, what is it, let me hear it," said Cali blowing the smoke in the air.

"It's my life story," she continued.

"I have an interesting story to tell," she said.

"Okay, let's hear it," said Cali, sitting up to listen to her.

◆ ◆ ◆

Later, that night. "Damn, we got to find this nigga Bagz," said Spank.

Donny replied. "We got to get him before he gets us."

Germane frowned. "Man, that nigga isn't built for no war." He sat on the passenger side.

"Let me tell you something, Germane, never underestimate your enemy, a scared man will kill you, and Bagz — he scared."

"When I see that motherfucker, I'm a pop his top," said Spank with a Tec-9 on his lap riding through Bagz's neighborhood. "This his hood right here, keep your eyes open," said Donny as they rode around looking for Bagz. He sat in the back seat.

The neighborhood was crowded, with hustlers, kids, gamblers, and corner stores. Spank slowed down and noticed a group of gangsters hanging out by the mailbox.

"If them motherfuckers ride past one more time, I'm a start blasting," said Nate.

Spank saw the unfamiliar faces and grew upset.

"Damn man, where this nigga at," Spank screamed and pressed the gas.

Donny said, "He probably hiding somewhere," sitting in the backseat.

"I am ready to shoot any of these mother fuckers," said Germane riding the passenger side and staring at a few thugs walking across the street.

"Chill G, we don't need to draw no unnecessary heat on us. We going to get him," said Donny.

"We out then, I'm about to go back up South Philly, we'll bump into his punk ass, sooner or later," said Spank.

Donny put his gun to the back of Germane's head. He blew his brains out. Blood splattered the window. "You stupid fuck. I told you to murder Tosha. You idiotically decided to let her live. Now if we get caught, we will go down for good." He fired another shot into Germaine's chest as Spank continued to speed away.

26

HOMICIDE HEADQUARTERS

Detectives Carves and Roberts sat in their joint office, surrounded by evidence boards and files from the Midnight Slasher investigation.

Carves leaned forward, analyzing the victim data.

"Let's start by looking at what these victims have in common," he said, determined. "We must identify a connection, something that binds them together and could lead us to the perpetrator."

Roberts nodded, staring at the victim images.

Carves wrote their findings on a notepad. "Reverend Franklin and his wife were active members of the community, well-respected in the church," he summarized.

"Fred Adams, a local businessman, and Kareem Thomas, a college student. We'll investigate. Is there a specific commonality we missed?"

They examined church records, databases, and testimonies.

"Reverend Don Franklin was a prominent member of the congregation, and the other victims had church affiliations."

Roberts tapped the table, thinking. "They all attended the same church," he shouted, realizing. "No coincidence. The Midnight Slasher may be targeting that crowd."

Carves was fascinated. "You're right. We may find the Slasher's purpose or a lead."

Detective Carves and Roberts knew their next step in solving the Midnight Slasher's riddle would take them to the chapel. The revelation that all of the victims had ties to the group motivated them to find answers within its confines.

It was located on the corner of 69th & Ogontz.

Carves and Roberts felt humility and calm in the church. The sacred place was dark, but the building seemed peaceful. Pastor Johnson met the detectives at the office.

"Good afternoon, gentlemen," Pastor Johnson said. "Can I help?"

Carves offered his hand professionally. "Detective Carves, Detective Roberts. We're investigating the Midnight Slasher case and suspect the church and its former members are involved."

Nodding, Pastor Johnson's' face darkened. "I am aware of the previous victims' affiliations with this church. They died tragically."

Carves leaned forward, watching the pastor. "Reverend Don Franklin was essential to this congregation. We need to know if there were unresolved difficulties, conflicts, or possible motives for these murders."

Pastor Johnson paused, saying. "I'm new here, but I'll help. However, speak to Sandra Williams. She knew Reverend Franklin personally and may have more information pertinent to your research."

The detectives looked at one other, excited to talk to someone who knew the former pastor. "Thank you, Pastor Johnson, for your help."

Pastor Johnson considered, "Sandra Williams was quite involved in the church community. She used to lead Wednesday night prayers. I haven't seen her in months but when she arrives, I'll give you detectives a call."

Carves and Roberts nodded, appreciating the pastor's idea. "Pastor Johnson, thanks. We'll be expecting your call."

◆ ◆ ◆

Spank took a sigh of relief.

"Damn, you were starving?" He slammed the bowl on the table. "That was scrumptious." He rose to his feet. "So, you are getting rid of me, huh?" he asked while hugging Lisa with both of his hands on her soft butt cheeks.

"Come see me tomorrow, Spank, oh, by the way, you got two hundred dollars to get my hair done, it's your fault, and you're the one who messed it up."

"Oh, that's how you feel," Spank said, reaching into his pocket and pulling out a stack of money wrapped in a rubber band. "Here, go get your shit done," he peeled off a hundred dollars and gave it to Lisa.

"Thank you," she hugged him.

He grabbed her thighs.

"Okay, now go before you make me miss my appointment."

"I'll holla at you," Spank said, walking out the door.

"I'm about to wife her young ass," he said, strolling towards the Maserati.

Lisa dialed Bagz's number. "Hello, Spank just left."

◆ ◆ ◆

Spank looked both ways with his hand on his gun searching for cops. Looking both ways once more, he climbed inside his SUV. He placed his gun on his lap and started the engine.

His windshield cracked from a bullet. Spank looked through his rearview mirror and saw five gangsters running up to his car with guns in their hands. "Oh shit," he grabbed his gun and aimed at the back window.

Long sparks blazed through the barrow of a machine gun. Spank's body shook from bullets tapping against the car door. "Y'all want a war?!" He shot back five times, then fumbled with his gun from hand to hand.

Spank felt sharp pains in his back. "Fuck yawl," he said, trying to start the ignition.

Masked shooters ran up to his driver-side window. He shot a bullet into the gunman's stomach. Then he fell to his knees.

More hooded gangsters began to surround the Maserati, shooting inside. Blood leaked from his mouth. He screamed as his body began to jerk back and forth from being filled with bullet holes.

He held on to his gun and shot one more time. He closed his eyes, not wanting to die, just trying to take the pain as more bullets began to puncture his flesh. A hooded gangster opened the door wearing leather gloves, placed his gun to Spank's head, and pulled the trigger.

Blood sprayed the passenger window before it shattered into pieces. The gunfire halted once they noticed Spank's brains on the passenger seat.

They all went running to the getaway cars as Lisa stood staring out the window.

27

Temptation's Shadows

Ecstasy stepped out of the corner store, a bag of snacks in hand. She wore her favorite outfit. The sun started to set to the sound of car horns.

Today, her focus was elsewhere, and she chose to tune out the noise, eager to return home.

She was about to enter the front door when a familiar automobile sped up next to her.

Bagz, her former flame, leaned over from the driver's seat, "Ecstasy, let me holla at you real' quick?"

Curiosity got the better of her, "Leave me the fuck alone. What do you want Bagz?" and Ecstasy paused, facing Bagz as he poured his heart out.

"I'm so sorry for everything but I miss you."

"I'm not doing this no more Bagz," she remained firm, declining his advances.

As Bagz watched Ecstasy turn to walk away, a chill ran

down his spine. Bagz couldn't get rid of the feeling that someone was watching him. He looked up and focused on the third-floor window's blinds, they started to shake rapidly.

Bagz was disappointed driving away.

Ecstasy hastily entered, closing the door behind her.

As she pushed open the door to her grandmother Helen's room, Ecstasy inhaled deeply. "Good morning."

"Good morning my grandchild," Grandma Helen was still laying on the bed.

The familiar scent of lavender filled the air, instantly calming her nerves. The room's lace curtains let soft sunshine pass through.

Ecstasy's eyes caught sight of a photograph of her mother and grandmother, "Look at you two looking so young," said Ecstasy, taking a seat on the edge of the bed. Ecstasy closed her eyes, allowing her mind to drift back to her childhood.

The memories of her mother's abuse resurfaced, like venomous snakes slithering through her thoughts.

"No mommy no," Ecstasy yelled as her mother clenched her fists, her nails digging into her palms, "AAHHH!" the pain grounding her into the present.

"Grandma," Ecstasy whispered, her voice trembling with a mixture of fear and determination. "I have to understand."

"What's wrong my dear?"

The room was silent as if the walls were holding their breath in anticipation of her grandmother's reply. And then, a gentle breeze rustled the curtains.

She continued with Ecstasy, her voice getting louder.

"I've carried the weight of my mother's actions for so long."

Ecstasy's eyes began to bubble up with tears that were about to roll down her cheeks. And then, as if in response to her plea, a sense of peace washed over Ecstasy.

"You must find fortitude and forgiveness. Your mom lost her way in life," said Grandma Helen.

"I endured my share of pain. After seeing my daughter fall into darkness, I fought to save you from suffering the same fate.

Ecstasy said, "I will not let my mother's behavior influence how I lived out my life."

"I'm so proud of you. My grandchild is all grown up now."

Grandma Helen's sleepy eyes closed.

Ecstasy felt a sense of closure. The weight of secrets and anguish left the room.

With a final glance at her mother's picture, Ecstasy whispered, "Thank you, Grandma Helen. And I will find a way to break free from the shadows that have haunted me for far too long."

Grandma Helen's eyes opened aggressively.

Only the faint sound of wind rustling through the open window could be heard in Grandma Helen's eerie room. Ecstasy, with her dark gaze and an air of mystery, sat across from her grandmother, Grandma Helen.

"Live your life. No one will harm you now." Grandma Helen's weathered face reflected years of wisdom and experience.

She leaned forward, her eyes filled with concern as she addressed her granddaughter, a lingering sadness in her voice. "Ecstasy, my love, I recognize the suffering you've had with Bagz. However, staying in that sadness will simply confine your spirit."

Ecstasy moaned as she set her eyes on an area outside the window. "Bagz had brought me joy and sadness in equal measure, leaving scars on my heart. Getting out of this loop feels difficult and nearly impossible."

Grandma Helen's voice had a forceful undertone to it. "Bagz's life will turn into a never-ending nightmare, full of the repercussions of his decisions. But my child, you have the power to reclaim your happiness. Stop allowing him to have a negative influence on your life."

Grandma Helen extended her wrinkly hand to Ecstasy, giving her comfort as well as support. "I can sense, there's a new chapter waiting to be written in your life. an opportunity to patch up the cracks and find a love that endures. The new guy you met recognizes the light you possess. Permit yourself to experience joy once more and to let love find you."

"I will try, Grandma," she whispered, her voice tinged with determination. "I'll put the heartache behind me and embrace the future. Bagz will never have the power to ruin my life again."

◆ ◆ ◆

Ecstasy sat across from Cali. It was in Cali's presence that she found solace and the courage to envision a brighter future.

The cozy café provided a sanctuary from the outside world, where their whispered conversations could remain intimate and protected. The aroma of freshly brewed coffee filled the space, blending with the casual hum of voices.

With a deep breath, Ecstasy began to share the depths of her emotions, her voice soft yet resolute.

Ecstasy confided in Cali as he touched her hands while remaining silent and supportive, realizing the weight she was carrying.

Ecstasy continued, her voice getting louder with each word, "I want to leave Philly. Finding a location where I can rebuild my life on my terms."

A flicker of excitement danced in Cali's eyes as he squeezed Ecstasy's hands, a sign of encouragement and unity. "Me, too, I understood the desire for a fresh start, the yearning to leave behind what was left of heartache and forge a path toward happiness. That's was up"

Cali said, "Together," his voice filled with certainty. "We can create a future far removed from the pain of our pasts. A place where love and healing can flourish."

Hope filled Ecstasy's heart as she locked eyes with Cali. In their presence, she felt a newfound strength, a belief that she could rewrite her narrative and embrace the love and happiness she deserved.

As they continued to discuss their shared dreams and aspirations, the weight of her past began to disappear.

With Cali by her side, she felt she could face any challenge, and overcome any obstacle.

Ecstasy and Cali emerged from the coffee shop holding hands, their hearts in harmony and overflowing with optimism. Philly would quickly fade into the past, serving as a stop on their way to a better future.

The next day

"Ever since I met you, my life has been good," said Ecstasy. She enjoyed Cali's company.

"I'm having the time of my life." Cali didn't respond.

He was in a daze staring at the ceiling of his hotel room. Ecstasy sensed a problem, "may I ask what is wrong with you?"

"I'm good. Why, you ask me that?" He didn't realize how different he was acting.

"All day you haven't been your regular happy self."

"Okay, you got me I'm in a jam. I'm working on my new book, and I have writer's block. My publishers are breathing down my back. But nothing I seem to write is good enough."

Ecstasy thought hard, "I have a good story for you to write."

"I'm serious, and you are playing games," he said, shaking his head. He lit up a cigarette.

"I'm not playing, and it would be perfect."

"Okay, what is it, let me hear it," said Cali blowing the smoke in the air.

"It's my life story," she continued. "I have an interesting story to tell," she said.

"Okay, let's hear it," said Cali, sitting up to listen to her.

28

Come Up

"What's wrong with you now, Cali?" Ecstasy asked slurping on her fruit juice. They were driving in his Jaguar and listening to old classic R&B. "You have been on some other shit."

Cali was stressed out and it showed on his face.

"Now." Cali laughed. "Why did you say that?"

"Because I know when you got something on your mind because you start acting all strange and you start getting quiet with that same look on your face."

"You think you know me too well," he said, taking a deep breath.

"Why won't you just say what's on your mind?" Cali hesitated for a few seconds then he parked by the Donut Shop on Broad & Master. "I was thinking, me and you have been together for a little while and it feels like I've known you all my life," he said, staring into her pretty eyes. "All I'm trying to say is that when I come home to my telly, I want to see you there. When I wake up in the morning, I want to see you lying next to me."

Ecstasy said, "I feel what you say." She stared at his Gucci watch. "Honestly, I love being with you, and would love to move in with you but my grandmom needs me there. I can't just leave her like that. We will have plenty of time when we leave Philly." She shook the hair from the side of her face with a slight turn of the neck. "You know how I feel about my grandma."

The left side of Cali's face moved up slightly. "Don't worry about all that, keep the key, you can come and go as you please like you have been doing."

He releases a deep breath of tension. Cali was trying to get ideas for his book. His publisher has been putting him under pressure. "That's what I'm talking about." He looked through his rear-view mirror and saw that the coast was clear. Then he drove up Master Street.

Ecstasy leaned over to kiss him while he drove. Her soft lips touched his cheek. "You are so sweet," she said in her baby voice. She kissed his cheek again and rubbed him. "He misses me?"

Cali remained calm as he drove.

Ecstasy's phone begins to ring.

"Don't answer it, baby," said Cali. "

"It might be my grandma," said Ecstasy. She looked down at her iPhone and couldn't recognize the phone number. "Who the hell is this?"

"I don't know, you might as well answer it now," said Cali.

Please don't let this be Bagz. She hoped. "Hello." "Ecstasy? It's me, Pebbles."

Thank God. "Pebbles? Where have you been?" she said excitedly.

Cali frowned his face.

"I'm at the mall in the parking lot. I need to tell you something important."

"Okay, what mall?" Ecstasy looked at Cali. "Just meet me at the Cheltenham Mall and don't tell nobody that you talked to me." Pebbles hung up.

"Okay, I'm on my way. Hello?"

"Ecstasy, are you okay? Who was that? Pebbles?"

"Cali, I need you to take me, to the Cheltenham Mall to meet her."

"Damn ma, I was going to cook dinner for you tonight," he said making a U-turn. "Then afterward you were going to be my desert." He shook his head.

"Ooh, well how about we skip dinner and dessert and I come home tonight and be your late-night snack?"

"You know what, I'm with that."

❖ ❖ ❖

Pebbles sat in her rental car waiting for Ecstasy. "There she goes, right there," she said after seeing Cali's Jaguar pull into the parking lot. Pebble's phone began to ring.

"Hello."

"Where you at, I'm here," said Ecstasy.

"I see you, just get out of the car, I will beep the horn."

"Okay, bye," said Ecstasy, hanging up the phone.

Ecstasy kissed Cali on the lips. "I'll see you tonight boo because I got my key." She flashed the keys he had given her in front of him. "See, I made you smile."

Ecstasy stepped out of the car. "Well, I will see you tonight."

"I'll be waiting for you," said Cali with a mysterious look in his eyes.

◆ ◆ ◆

Tosha was moved to a new home with the help of Bagz so he decided to check up on her.

The sound of the doorbell caught her attention. She stood by two guys that pull out a Glock.40s and cocked it back. She walked towards the door. She peeked through the peephole and saw Bagz standing there with army fatigue pants, Timberland boots, and a black ACG hoody on.

He was staring at his phone.

"Tosha! I know you in there." he said.

She placed her gun on her pantie line and closed her robe. "It's Bagz," she said after looking through the peephole.

His presence made her feel good. She opened the door. "Hey, brother."

"Tosha, Hey... How' you been?" Bagz said handing her a dozen roses from behind his back.

Tosha gave him a passionate hug. "Thank you, Bagz, for helping me find this penthouse. These are my cousins who come to watch my back. That home invasion almost took my life. That shit ain't going down no more!" She watched Bagz walk past her into her living room, then she closed the door.

"I've been calling you for days, what's up with you?"

"Have a seat Bagz, I have to tell you something." Bagz took a seat next to Tosha as she began to speak.

"Yesterday, I found some drugs to keep the business going. I got my family to be my muscle. Then you as a shield but bro, did you give them our address?"

"Hell, no they already had me and Stephone cribs on a scope. For now, you stay close to me, okay," he said, wiping her tears. "You know we took care of them niggas who set Stephon up. Spank is dead. You never have to worry about him again." His dead body flashed in Bagz's head. He started feeling guilty.

"Thank you, Bagz," she said in tears.

"Germane got killed. It wasn't us though." She rested her head on Bagz's shoulders. "Stephon was a good man."

"We were getting money. They fucked up my plug. I don't have no product left."

"I might help you with that."

"What' you mean?"

She walked away as Bagz followed behind.

"Where are you going?"

"He used to tell me that his enemies would eventually hunt

him down and kill him."

She pulled out her gun.

"Aye, what you are doing?" Bagz asked, shocked.

Tosha took a few steps back. "Stephon said that if something was to happen to him, then I should leave some money for his family and the rest was for me. For ME!"

She paused and let out a few tears. She dropped to her knees and dropped the gun on the floor.

Bagz stepped in and picked up the gun.

He pushed the release, pulled the clip out, and took a bullet out of the chamber. "You don't need this."

Tosha began screaming. "Fuck you, Germane! I'm glad you're dead!"

Bagz tried hard to get Tosha under control. He dropped to his knees and hugged her. "Just chill Tosha. Breath baby."

Tosha took deep breaths.

"Tosha, you, ok?" Asked her cousins.

"I'm good. Give me a minute."

"Wait right here?"

Bagz took a minute to answer.

The ceiling fans cooled the room.

She walked up to the safe and turned the knob to the right, leaving it open.

Bagz stood in the other room waiting.

Tosha opened the six-foot-tall safe. She stared at the big

piles of cash. Tosha remained silent as she opened the combination to the safe. She began to gasp after seeing millions of dollars in cash and kilos of cocaine.

She came back with a bag with ten keys in it. "Remember you told me to save up because this shit doesn't last forever?"

"Yea when you first got with Stephon, I told you that," Bagz said in deep concentration.

"Well let's just say I've been saving for a rainy day." She threw the bag at Bagz. He caught it with his chest and opened it.

"What the fuck, is it my birthday?" Bagz's eyebrows raised to the top of his head, and he hugged Tosha. "Listen, Tosha, from now on, you don't have to worry about shit!" he said loudly.

29

Inside the club

"Be careful," said Pebbles as she and Ecstasy made their way to the bar looking sexy in their outfits. "Let me get two Sex on the beaches," said Pebbles and took seats behind the bar.

Tone appeared from behind Pebbles. Tone saw an empty table. "Come on let's go over there where we can be in private."

◆ ◆ ◆

"I can't believe you got me up in this nut-ass club." Donny didn't like going to clubs and being caught up in the crowd.

"Drinks on me bitch!" said his girlfriend Kelly and tossed three hundred ones in the air.

◆ ◆ ◆

On the other side of the club

Tosha stood with her bodyguard cousins, Taymar and Franky on the side of her. Then Bagz arrived.

"What the hell is he doing here?" Ecstasy said.

Bagz smiled at Ecstasy. Now was his time to talk to her.

"Bagz, don't look now, but Donny is here, he sees us and he's calling someone on the phone," said Tosha.

Bagz's heart tingled, he wanted Donny's head on a silver platter.

Everyone started freaking out. Bagz couldn't forget about being kidnapped and beaten by this guy. And Tosha remembers hearing his name that night and began to have flashbacks.

Shadows of the Past

Tosha found herself in anxiety.

Donny, one of the men who had killed Stephon, now stood across the room, his presence sending shivers down her spine. Memories of the painful past resurfaced, reminding her of how he had robbed her and taken the life of her boyfriend, Stephon. The scars, both physical and emotional, were still written deeply within her.

"Tosha, are you ok?" Bagz knew how she felt.

Tosha's heart raced, her mind clouded with a mix of fear and willpower. She was aware that she had to move quickly. "Excuse me, I have to use the bathroom," she rose from the table, she discreetly made her way towards the club's bathroom, hoping to find a moment of solace and privacy. Her cousins stood by the woman's bathroom door.

When she was inside, she inhaled deeply to center herself before grabbing her phone.

Tosha dialed the number she had committed to memory with quivering hands: that of Detectives Carves and Roberts, the devoted detectives who had helped her through the traumatic events following Stephon's murder.

The phone rang, the seconds stretching long, until finally, a voice answered on the other end.

The voice said, "Detective Carves speaking," with professionalism and care.

"This is Tosha. We spoke at the hospital when my boyfriend Stephon died." Tosha communicated the crucial information with trembling in her voice.

"Sure, how can I help you?"

"I just spotted the guy at the club. He's at Club Dancers. Please, something needs to be done. The one who killed Stephon."

Detective Carve's tone changed to one of seriousness as he realized the gravity of the situation. "Keep your cool, Tosha. We're moving forward. Don't challenge him. We'll take care of everything while you find a secure hiding location."

She left the restroom with newfound energy, looking for a place where she might relax while she waited for the police to show up.

Outside, a sense of urgency penetrated the air as Detective Carves and Roberts, accompanied by a team of uniformed officers, swiftly made their way to the club. The detectives were well aware of the danger Donny posed, given his criminal history and the violent nature of his actions.

Carves gave his squad the required directions as they drew near the door, assuring a well-organized operation.

The music and laughter that had filled the club now faded into the background as the detectives prepared to apprehend Donny.

Inside, Tosha frantically combed through the crowd in search of Donny. She texts Carves, Donny's location and description. Moments later, the door burst open, flooding the club with a sudden influx of uniformed officers. Panic and confusion ensued as people scattered.

Donny caught off guard, attempted to blend in with the chaos, but the experienced eyes of Detective Carves and Roberts were quick to spot him. In a matter of seconds, the detectives closed in, "Donny, you're under arrest!" Detective Carver's voice cut through the commotion, commanding and firm, leaving no room for escape.

"I ain't do shit!" Donny's face twisted in a mixture of defiance and panic as he realized he had been backed into a corner. As the officers apprehended him, he glanced in Tosha's direction, their eyes locking for a brief moment.

Tragic Moment

The next week, Tone stood outside his house, surrounded by his friends, Tosha, Pebbles, and Tanisha. As they swapped tales and enjoyed the warm summer evening, laughter filled the air. It was a moment of respite from the harsh realities of their lives, a fleeting oasis of friendship.

Unexpectedly, a car rushed by them as its tires rumbled against the road. They looked up, startled, to see the car driving away down the street. Before they could understand what was happening, the sound of bullets took the place of the screeching of wheels.

"Rat bitch!" The car's voice screamed out, its words tinged with dread and a sickening intention. The air filled with the unmistakable pops of gunfire as the car unleashed a torrent of bullets toward Tone and his friends.

"Oh my God," said Tosha who had dove behind a parked car.

Pebbles and Tanisha, caught in the line of fire, were struck by the hail of bullets. Pebbles, unable to escape the onslaught, fell to the ground, life slipping away from her before help could arrive.

"Pebbles!" Tone yelled.

Tanisha, who was hurt but was still battling, struggled to stay alive.

"What's up fuck boys!" With determination etched on his face, Tone drew his weapon and returned fire, aiming at the fleeing car. Shots rang out into the night, but the car vanished into it, leaving nothing but the echoes of violence behind it.

The sirens wailed, growing louder as emergency responders rushed to the scene. The formerly tranquil area was changed into a spectacle of agony and despondency.

"Pebbles Don't Die!" Tone was in shock. He finally walked away after hearing cop sirens. Neighbors emerged from their homes, their faces etched with shock and horror at the sight before them.

30

The World Is Coming to a Massacre

Pebbles laid in her casket with a white dress on that made her look like a princess. Boyz II Men's classic, End of the Road has been played in the background. Her death saddened her family and friends that attended the funeral. In the long line of those waiting to pay their last respect was Tyson, followed by Ecstasy, Tosha, and Cali. Tone took it the hardest he was dying inside but remained a cool image. They were all devastated by the tragedy. Tanisha's mother, Jackie, was in tears from the loss of Pebbles, but grateful to still have Tanisha alive in critical condition.

Tone held a dozen roses and placed them on her casket.

The next couple of days

"This one for you sis," said Tone. He was smoking a blunt reminiscing. "I'm going to kill whoever did this!" Tone was furious about the entire situation. Losing Pebbles and Tanisha was a major hit to his consciousness and has started causing violent reactions to the streets. He was at a point of no return.

Any problem Bagz had, Tone handled it, causing mayhem and chaos on the streets. If money was owed to Bagz or any disrespect, Tone would hunt them down and kill them. He wanted nothing but revenge for the death of his sister, Pebbles.

The murders he was committing were becoming uncontrollable and Bagz had to throw a meeting to calm down the violence.

◆ ◆ ◆

Bagz drove up to the Recreational Center to meet with Tone. Bagz exited his Porsche SUV and headed inside the playground. Tone stood by the entrance surrounded by a group of gangsters. Bagz approached Tone with hugs and handshakes.

"Let me holla at you real quick big homey." Bagz and Tone stepped to the side, so none could eavesdrop on their conversation. "What's on your mind, Bagz?" Tone knew Bagz was concerned about the way he was handling business.

"Tone, you got to calm down. You are bringing a lot of unnecessary heat on us. You are leaving dead bodies all over the place."

"Well, what can I say? I'm good at my job."

"You can go to jail but don't put the rest of us in danger."

"What' you want me to do? Let niggas disrespect

you? I'm making examples out of these niggas because when they fuck with you, they got to fuck with me. These Basterds killed my sister."

"I understand that and ever since Stephon got killed, these mother fuckas think they don't have to pay. I'm a get that money they owe him and me."

"That's why I do, what I do."

"But you got to make your killings clean, it's getting too noisy, make the bodies disappear. You can't get charged with murder on a missing person, you feel me?"

"All right, I got you."

"You think you can handle that?"

"Of course."

"Okay, well, the boy' E-Money from southwest owes me thirty thousand."

"Oh, yeah? I got him don't worry."

Bagz handed him a cut-off piece of paper, "This is the address to his seafood store. You can find him there."

"Say no more."

Bagz shook his head in disagreement.

Relentless Pursuit

Bagz could not shake the memories of his time with Ecstasy. "Im'a get her back watch," he said getting dressed.

He thought their bond was too strong to be entirely severed. "She got to miss me. I'm that nigga." He started by writing sincere text messages, remembering their shared experiences and their earlier joy.

She ignored his text as he poured his heart out on the message, hoping Ecstasy would feel the same way.

Ecstasy opened her front door one day and Bagz was standing there with a dozen of roses. "I just wanted to give you these," without another word she slammed the door in his face.

Later that night, she lay side by side with Cali. Her body was with him but her mind was on the other side of town.

Late one evening, Bagz appeared outside Ecstasy's home again, unable to contain his feelings any longer. "I swear to make up for my mistakes."

The thought of giving him another chance tugged at her heartstrings, despite the risks.

With a heavy sigh, she raced to her front door. "I need for you, not to come here again," then slowly closed the door.

31

I Declare War

"Across town "I'm going to the strip club!" yelled Bagz excitedly. A thousand thoughts raced through his head. His navigation system announced his arrival as he parked across the street from the exotic nightclub. He stared through his tinted window at an attractive young female.

"Damn, she looks just like Ecstasy." Not feeling like getting out of the car to fetch for whores, he simply beeped the horn. He watched the fine young bunny as she talked to a potential customer. He grew agitated and beeped the horn again, rolling his window down.

"Yeer!" Bagz yelled, catching her attention. "Come here."

"Who? Me?" she asked blushing, observing Bagz's Yukon truck sitting on twenty-six-inch rims. "I got to see who this is," she said to the man she was with. "Excuse me for a minute, I'll be back."

"Oh, it's like that? Go ahead then, it's plenty more fish in the sea, you little guppy." The man said angrily.

Bagz sat in his truck smiling from ear to ear as he watched the stripper walk towards him. "Damn ma, I know you're cold, get in."

"Where do I know you from?"

"Maybe a past life or something, I'm trying to holler at you though, get in," Bagz demanded as she walked around to the passenger seat, opened the door, slid in, and made herself comfortable.

"Damn, you a sexy motherfucker." Bagz flirted, pulling off into the expressway.

◆ ◆ ◆

An hour later

"I don't know about this," said Bagz. He was parked in front of the Blumberg project buildings before the city knocked them down.

"Nothing going to happen," said Kim.

"Let's go to the hotel."

"I told you my daughter is in there sleeping by herself. I know I'm a bad mother, but I need the money."

Bagz shook his head. "All right, come on," he said then hopped out of the car.

◆ ◆ ◆

16th floor "For you to be living in the projects, you got this shit looking like a penthouse." Bagz turned on the radio to the quiet storm. In between the Sheets by the Isley Brothers played through the room. "You have nice taste." She complimented Bagz, observing the expensive sneakers on his feet.

"This is how I'm living, nothing but the best." Bagz pulled out a pocket of money. "Dance for me, Kim."

Kim began to move her hips and waist to the rhythm of the song. "That's what I'm talking about." Bagz had a smile on his face.

Bagz relaxed on the bed, watching Kim dance. "Do you have any weed?"

"Can Michael Jordan slam dunk?"

"I guess that means yes." They both laughed.

Bagz sprinkled some loud in a Swisher and rolled a blunt. He sparked it up and the two got high as a jet. Kim began licking Bagz's neck, getting him aroused as he lifted her and laid her on the bed. Then they began to indulge in foreplay. He laid on his back as Kim climbed on top of him and began to ride him like a wild cowgirl. He held a firm grip on her soft ass, moving her in and out of his joystick.

"You like it?" She moaned.

"You feel really good right now. Damn girl." He stroked in and out of her. The bed was squeaking, and her headboard was knocking on the wall. "Make me," Kim screamed.

"Do what you got to do." Bagz lifted his hips, hitting her g-spot.

"Aw, I'm," Kim screamed, biting her lips to hold back her scream. Her body jumped like a bolt of lightning hit her, and she exploded with passion.

30 minutes later

"Come on Kim, let's get in the shower," Bagz said, standing up.

"Okay, let's go." She led him to the bathroom and stepped her flawless body into the shower.

◆ ◆ ◆

The steam from the hot water made the mirrors foggy. The night was cold, and the sky was pitch black with glowing stars decorating the heavens. He cut the water off and dried it off. Kim followed him to the bed and cut the lights out.

The quiet storm entertained their ears as they slept.

The only light in the room was from their phones, which were plugged into a socket on the wall. Bagz's eyes slowly eased open and closed again as a thumping sound startled them.

"What was that?" Bagz asked. *This bitch trying to set me up. I'm tripping. I don't even know this bitch and I'm sleeping with her?*

"I just heard something coming from over there," Kim said. "Aunt Sherry?" she yelled. "It's probably my aunt coming home from work."

Bagz grew paranoid. "I got a few runs to make." "This late?"

◆ ◆ ◆

Bagz headed out the door. His eyes darted around the cramped hallway as he waited for the elevator doors to open. He boarded the elevator and hit the button for the bottom floor. Every floor of the flight was riddled with danger making the trip tense.

Bagz emerged from the north Philadelphia project building with his heart racing and the weight of the pistol around his waist. Although he was conscious of the risk he took, he was unable to resist the temptation.

"You got some work?" said the junkie who approached him. His eyes were hazy and erratically moving. The man urged Bagz to sell him some narcotics, "get the fuck outa' my face," said Bagz pulling out his gun, and making an effort to leave.

The man walked away in a different direction. Bagz kept watching his back but still felt he was being followed. He accelerated his steps until he finally made it to his car and breathed deeply, feeling some relief.

However, just as he was ready to turn the key, what looked like the Midnight Slasher, who was dressed all in black with a black mask on, emerged from behind a tree.

Bagz froze as his attacker attempted to open his car door, feeling his heart in his throat. Bagz rolled down the window with shaking hands. Bagz slid down the window and raised his handgun with shaking hands, but his shot missed the assailant.

Bagz's mind was racing as he tried to understand what had just transpired as he stepped on the throttle pedal with an adrenaline rush. He was terrified and uneasy, but he was also confident that he had made it through another night in north Philadelphia.

◆ ◆ ◆

A week later

"Take me home Cali."

"I will not, you need to be with me where it's safe."

"No, take me home now. I want to see my grandmom before we leave."

"Ecstasy, let's talk about this."

"No, take me home now Cali," she raised her voice. "Okay, okay, let's go."

Cali drove in silence.

Cali pulled up to Ecstasy's grandmother's house and parked.

The street was silent and empty as Cali made his way to Ecstasy's home. Cali didn't mind that the neighborhood was dark and the sun had long set. Ecstasy was someone he was eager to see and spend time with.

Cali became aware of a change as he got closer to the house. The entrance door was slightly ajar, and the interior lights were flickering.

Ecstasy opened the door as Cali entered the room and immediately had a chill down his spine. There was an odd aroma in the air, and the home was strangely silent.

"I'm home grandma," Ecstasy called her but didn't get a response to her call.

"She's probably sleeping so let's stay quiet."

"For sho', where is the bathroom?" Cali asked.

"Upstairs to the left," said Ecstasy.

As he made it upstairs, he abruptly noticed a sound coming from the bathroom. Cali moved cautiously in the direction of the noise.

"What was that?"

That's when he opens the bathroom door and noticed a dark figure in front of him. It was an elderly woman dressed in vintage attire. He fell backward, nearly tripping over his own feet. Despite his best efforts, he was unable to leave the room because he was ensnared there.

Cali thought his eyes were playing tricks on him. He stared into the bathroom and ceased to move before the dark figure dissipated into nothingness.

◆ ◆ ◆

Cali struggled for breath as he made his hasty exit from the restroom. Being free of the eerie figure made him feel better.

Ecstasy yelled upstairs, "Cali, are you ok?"

Cali made his way back to the living room.

"Yes," he said, hugging Ecstasy and kissing her on the forehead. "Ecstasy, I will be back in the morning."

"Why what happened."

"Something just came up. I'll be back in the morning."

"Okay Cali, promise me you're going to call me."

Ecstasy sucked on Cali's bottom lip and said, "I love you," she said blowing a kiss at him and watching him walk out the door.

Ecstasy entered her grandmother's room and hung her pocketbook up on the hat rack. "Grandma!" She yelled.

"Girl, why are you yelling so loud in my room," said Ms. Helen.

"Oh, I thought you weren't here."

"Well, what's wrong?"

"Another one gets murdered by some sick lunatic serial killer."

"I told you when you first moved here to not get attached to these hoodlums. All they do is shoot each other up and have babies and leave mothers to raise a bastard child."

"I can't take this anymore, me and Cali's moving to Hollywood and you going with us."

"Don't be silly. I'm not going anywhere. I'm trapped here forever."

"Grandmom, why are you trapping yourself here?"

"It's not that simple," Grandma Helen explained.

"But grand mom, you're all I have. I need you."

"I wish I could, but you're a young adult now so go ahead and explore life. This is not a good place for you. It's too dangerous here for you. Yes, I have a bad feeling that if you don't leave soon then your life will be in jeopardy, and I don't want to see anything bad happen to you. So go," said Grandma Helen as

UMAR QUADEER

she kissed Ecstasy on the forehead

32

INSIDE THE CHURCH

On Wednesday, Carves and Roberts finally received the phone call that they had been waiting on for a while.

"Okay, pastor. I'm already on my way. Carves took a few sips of his coffee. "Let's go, buddy. Sandra is at the church right now." Roberts and Carves ran as fast as they could from their office to the police cruiser.

The detectives joined the church's prayer circle.

During Sandra's leadership of the prayer, Detective Carves and Roberts went unnoticed. And to wrap everything up, she said, "We all have sinned, so we ask God for forgiveness and healing. Amen," she said, and as she stepped away from the microphone, she was greeted with cheers.

Immediately following the service, Carves, and Roberts went up to speak with Sandra Williams. When they introduced themselves, they said, "We are detectives investigating the Midnight Slasher cases, and we wanted any relevant information you may have about Reverend Don Franklin and his wife Riana."

Although Sandra's eyes widened, she did not lose her composure. "Reverend Franklin was a dear friend," she declared with both regret and resolve. "He was murdered and there were rumors of dissension and fighting within the church, but I never imagined that it would result in such a tragedy."

Carves stared with utter concentration. "Sandra, please share everything with us. Even the most insignificant detail could make or break this case."

Sandra inhaled and looked determined. She ran through in her head all of the tense situations and disagreements that were going on behind the scenes at the church.

"Even though I did wrong by getting so close to him. I would never, ever wish for their deaths," she said, referring to the situation.

Carves and Roberts glanced at one other, realizing the gravity of the news.

"Were you having an affair with the Reverend?"

"Was the Reverend your lover?"

Sandra's voice shook with reluctance. As she moved forward, Detective Carves' got anxious.

"Even I loved him," she admitted, choking back tears as she did so. "He told me everything about his wife's jealousy. She knew about the affairs. Him cheating. She even found out about me and Don's hotel nights. That woman was so strong. To put up with that. I thought she was going to kill somebody, the way she acted. They have been together for twenty years. The bond between us didn't last long. A year after both him and his wife were brutally killed."

"Sandra, do you know anyone who would do this to them?"

"It was also a lady by the name of Helen. He had the deepest feelings for her. He felt a deep love for her. Now those two uses to be seen everywhere. He even got caught having dinner with her. When his wife found out she ran up on her one night and said, 'If you don't leave my husband alone. I'll kill you bitch.'

Riana threatened to kill her if she didn't leave the town immediately."

The detective leaned in closer while maintaining a low but demanding tone. "Sandra, this information is critical to figuring out what happened." The victims deserve justice. So, what happened after that?"

"Helen disappeared after that. She could not be located. Maybe she's the one who killed them," she said as she wiped a tear from her face.

Following Sandra's report, the detective leaned back, interested in what she had to say. "Sandra, do you know who this is? This Helen. Where would we be able to find her?"

When asked who she was, Sandra replied, "Helen," but there was a hint of fear in her voice.

Carves and Roberts exchanged shocked glances with one another.

"She attends the church on rare occasions, on average once

a month. On the other hand, I haven't seen her since Riana allegedly made a threat against her. I've heard that Reverend Don purchased her a house on 16th Street by the fire station. That they shared in private, but other than that, I don't know anything further about it." She inhaled deeply and exhaled slowly. She felt better letting her secrets out.

"There are some things that Helen can tell you that I can't. Find her; she may have additional information about the things that Reverend Franklin was up to."

Detective Roberts scribbled down Helen's name in his notepad while his eyes met Carves with a fresh purpose.

Later, that night

"I got to get the fuck out of here!" Bagz raced up the street with his bags packed in the trunk. "Everybody on the run!" Thoughts were racing through his mind like the US Olympics. "What the hell is going on in my life? This is not how it is supposed to be," he said with the music blasting. "Damn!" he said racing through a red light.

He turned the wheel, dodging traffic. "Fuck!" An old lady in a Volkswagen came crashing into the back of his car causing him to spin out of control. His car came to a complete stop. Then he looked through his rear-view at who crashed into him. "Learn how to drive!" he yelled and stepped out of his car.

With a frown on his face, he noticed a cop car pulling up to the scene. "Aw shit," he said getting back into his car.

"Excuse me sir?" said the lady who had crashed into him. Bagz got in his car and pressed the gas. "Sir, I need to know who you are insured by!" she said but Bagz was already racing through the intersection. "Stupid son of a bitch!" said the old lady.

◆ ◆ ◆

The Charger was built for speed as it accelerated through two blocks at a fast pace. "I got to make it to the highway," he said watching the cop flash their lights behind him.

"I need backup. Need backup. Hit and run suspect in a Black charger with tinted windows. He is headed for the highway," said the aggressive police officer.

He was a hot head and moments like this boosted his adrenaline. He gave chase with his sirens on. "You're going to jail today."

By the time Bagz made it to the highway, he had five cop cars on his tail. "This is not happening to me right now!" He was reaching speeds of hundred and thirty miles per hour.

Bagz came up to the Fairmont exit.

"Change of plans motherfucker," he said heading to Fairmont Park. "I got to shake them off me."

He made it to Fairmont Park with police cars flashing their lights behind him. He rode on the pavement through the grass heading to a dead end of trees. "I know this park like the back of my hand." Bagz slammed on the brakes crashing into a tree. He popped the trunk and jumped out of the car. "Here they come," he yelled, observing cop cars closing in on him.

Bagz ran to the trunk and grabbed his Louis Vuitton gym bag filled with hundred-dollar bills. Then he reached down and grabbed a machine gun with an extended clip. "I'm not going to jail," he screamed as the police officers made their arrival. "I'm not putting my hands up!" he screamed, squeezed the trigger, and let off what seemed like Fourth of July fireworks.

Bagz aimed his gun at each cop car that pulled up in front of him. Rapid fire from his gun started busting windows and putting holes in the hood. Officers took cover while drawing their weapons. He backed up, fired, and then ran through a jungle of trees. He heard shots whistling past. He hoped not to get hit.

◆ ◆ ◆

Inside Ecstasy's house

"Hell?" she said as she walked into her living room. She flicked on the lights. "What a night." She headed up the flight of stairs.

"Ecstasy, is that you?" Grandma Helen asked.

"Yes, grand mom. I'm home."

"Are you okay? It's late."

"Yes," she said and flopped down on her bed.

Ecstasy started crying uncontrollably.

Grandma Helen peeked inside. "Can I come in baby?" she asked.

"Yes, you can," said Ecstasy, making room on the bed.

"Are you okay?"

"My life is a nightmare."

Grandma Helen ran her fingers through Ecstasy's hair and

wiped her tears. "In life, you lose friends and gain them just as quickly. That's why I always told you not to get attached to these people because it hurts when they are taken away. A lot of things had happened before you got here. A lot of things that I choose not to explain. I just want you to know that you're beautiful and whatever happens is meant to be."

Grandma Helen started rising to her feet to walk to the door.

Grandma Helen stopped in her tracks. "All questions are not meant to be answered." She closed the door with an evil grin.

Ecstasy got up from her bed and locked the door.

Then she raced towards the closet and began packing all her bags.

She yanked down her shirts from their hangers then reached on shelves, pulling down sweaters and designer shoes, and placed them in suitcases. "I got to go," she said emptying her dresser drawers into her luggage.

She sat on top of her suitcase and zipped it up. "Unbelievable," she said, noticing she left a shirt hanging up in the closet. She stepped inside and grabbed the shirt off the hanger. "What the hell," she screamed as something fell from the top shelf.

Ecstasy stared down at the huge dagger, willing it to disappear. "What the hell is this?"

The knife had dry blood on it.

"Did you lose something?" Grandma Helen asked standing behind Ecstasy.

"You scared me," Ecstasy said, kicking the knife out of eyes sight. "How did you get in here the door was locked."

"The lock on this door never works." Grandma Helen said with an evil grin. "I just wanted to tell you that I love you and I'm going to bed."

"Okay, good night grandma."

"Don't forget to wake me in the morning if you're leaving and I'm sleeping."

"You know I will." The two hugged. "You were always my favorite," said Grandma Helen heading back out the door.

Ecstasy's smile faded into fear as she closed the door. She took a chair from the corner of the room and placed it under the doorknob. She raced back to the dresser.

33

"Thump! Thump! Thump!"

A banging on her window startled her. She jumped, holding her chest.

"Thump! Thump!"

Ecstasy opened the curtains and saw Bagz hanging to the branches of the tree.

"What the hell are you doing up there?" she asked opening her window.

"Let me in Ecstasy, the cops are chasing me," Bagz begged.

"Come on boy," she said stepping to the side to allow Bagz to climb in.

"Oh, thank God you were home. I lost my phone in the park. You a lifesaver," Bagz said standing in Ecstasy's bedroom.

Ecstasy put her fingers on her lips. "Don't make no noise, my grandmother is still awake," she explained.

"Oh, my bad," said Bagz.

He had his bag strapped to his back.

"Okay."

"EX, I want you to run away with me."

"I don't have no time for games."

"I'm not playing, I got a bag full of money. We can go anywhere you want to go," he said exposing the bag of cash. Bagz stared around at, Ecstasy's room. "I see you packed, ready to go." He walked to the closet and grabbed the doorknob.

"Listen, Bagz, you are talking crazy. You know that me and Cali are leaving for California tomorrow." Bagz let go of the closet door.

"Please don't. I want you, baby. My days have been hell without you. The money. This war. It all took me away from you. But I thought about you every night. Then I realized I couldn't ruin your life, so I just stayed away." Bagz was stressed out. "This is not supposed to be happening. It's like I'm living in a movie." He walked to the bed and flopped down.

"Come here," he said, Ecstasy lay beside him.

"Today was a rough day. I'm trying not to think about it," he said comforting her. "I'm so tired, I can't keep my eyes open."

"You can't sleep here, what about Cali?"

"That chump isn't nobody, he was just borrowing what's mine." He kissed Ecstasy on her lips.

"We got to be quiet," she said as Bagz undressed her.

He kissed her neck and entered her from the side.

"You got the best that I ever had in my life," said Bagz taking strokes in and out of her soft wetness. "Mm, your ass is so soft."

Bagz held her tight in his arms and rubbed his fingers across her nipples.

"Bagz, Bagz, Bagz," she screamed in a low tone. The sound of her voice made the sex even better as he climaxed all inside of her.

Bagz dozed off and started dreaming about Ecstasy's grandmother.

With a nasty grin on her face, she asked, "Didn't I tell you never to come back here again?" Bagz tossed and turned in his sleep. He was experiencing a nightmare that was all too real.

In his dream, he was standing in a room that was shrouded in shadows. He turned to glance around and saw that he was still in Ecstasy's grandmother's home.

He turned when he heard a creaking sound and saw the elderly woman standing there. Her face was contorted into a frown, her eyes hollow and dark. She hissed, her voice full of hatred, "Did I not tell you never to come back here again?"

Bagz attempted to speak, but his throat felt tight and dry. In fear, all he could do was stare at the elderly woman.

The grandma kept gazing at him, her eyes penetrating deep into his being. Bagz experienced a chill down his spine and wanted to turn around and flee, but he was unable to move.

The elderly woman abruptly started to transform. Her hair started to fall out in clumps, and her skin turned gray and mottled. Her teeth turned into fangs, and her fingers lengthened and curled. As the beast pounced at him, its mouth gaping wide, Bagz shouted in horror.

◆ ◆ ◆

Ecstasy lay next to him in deep thought. Soon she started hearing Bagz snore. Then she started hearing whispers in her head. They gave her plenty of evil ideas for things to do to Bagz. They advised her to harm him. "Break his heart the same way he broke yours," said a voice.

Ecstasy's mind turned into a place where the voices of her grandma and her thoughts clashed. She made an effort to fight them, but they persisted. She started to experience a loss of control. She rose to her feet and walked towards the door then she looked at Bagz laying fast asleep and headed to the bathroom.

Tears rolled down her cheek as she ran some hot water for a bubble bath. *What will I tell Cali?* She thought.

Inside the bedroom, Bagz lay helplessly in Ecstasy's bed in deep sleep. The bedroom door slowly opened, and the Midnight entered. The serial killer walked towards the bed where Bagz was laying and looked down at him.

Breathing slowly and anticipating death, the masked murderer held the sharp dagger tight and firm.

Terror was in the air as the Midnight began humming Grandma Helen's favorite church song.

The smooth murder melody slowly woke Bagz up. He was still dreaming.

Bagz opened his eyes after stretching. When he looked up, he almost pissed his pants.

His heart dropped at the sight of the Midnight Slasher.

Black hoody with a black mask holding a knife.

"Fuck," he said wondering if his mind was playing tricks on him. He tried to reach for his gun. "I'm a pop you!" was the last words that Bagz got a chance to say before the Midnight slasher swung his knife so hard that when it hit Bagz's forehead, it went through the front and out the back. Bagz face showed pain. Syrupy blood squirted from Bagz's brains as the Midnight Slasher yanked his knife back out of his head.

The murderer looked down at Bagz and watched his life fade away.

Ecstasy sat inside her warm bubble bath reflecting on life. She rose her naked body out of the warm bubble bath and dried off. Wrapping the towel around her body, she walked into the bedroom. "Bagz, do you want me to make you something to eat," she asked while lying beside him.

"Okay well, get some rest and we can go." Ecstasy got comfortable under the covers and fell asleep.

8:00 am

Knock! Knock! Knock!

"Who the hell is that? Cali?" Ecstasy raced to her window and looked out front. "Oh no!"

The entire police district was in front of her door.

"Bagz, get up!" she shook his body. "What is going on!" she screamed. "Bagz get up." She lifted the blanket and noticed the huge knife wound on Bagz's chest with blood soaking the mattress. She looked down at herself and noticed that she too was covered in blood. She looked at the wall and Midnight was written in Bagz's blood.

"Grandma," she yelled, running towards her grandmother's room.

Knock! Knock! Knock!

"This is the police anybody home!"

"Grandma," she said knocking on Grandma Helen's bedroom door. She forced herself into her room. "Where are you?"

Inside Grandma Helen's room was gloomy and creepy. Candles were lit in the darkness. A wooden dresser that barely stood on its four legs welcomed Ecstasy inside for a closer look.

Grandma Helen emerged from the closet. "What are you doing in here?" Grandma Helen asked fixing her clothing.

"Grandma, what did you do? The police are at the door." Ecstasy asked, noticing a knife collection hanging from her closet door and black hooded robes hanging from hangers.

Detective Carves and Roberts stood outside screaming. "This is the police, I wanted to have words with the owner of this house." He glanced at the third-floor window.

"I see movement inside," said Carves.

Ecstasy said, "I'll answer it, you wait here."

She raced to the front door and opened it. Letting the sunshine in the dark-shaded house.

"Hello, I'm Detective Carves and Roberts. I'm here to speak with Helen."

"Grandma, the cops are here," Ecstasy cried. "They going

to take you away from me." She walked inside as the detectives followed. They stared at each other in amazement.

"What is that on your shirt?" Carves asked noticing blood stains all over her. "Are you here alone?"

"Just me my grandma Helen and my Boyfriend Bagz."

"Bagz?" The detectives said together. They drew their weapons and called for backup. "Hey!"

"Don't worry sweetie, everything is going to be all right." Said Carves.

"But grandma, why are you doing this to me?" Ecstasy asked.

"You must learn on your own. You must be your own woman."

The officers had guns in hand.

They moved in slowly with hand signals.

"Grandma, what is going on? Why did you do this?" Ecstasy grew emotional.

Grandma Helen closed her eyes. "You can't run from what life has to offer. You must deal with this to grow. You will get all the help you need."

"I'm not letting them take you away from me." Ecstasy grabbed her hands.

"Put your hands behind your back!" officers yelled, with Ecstasy in point-blank range.

Ecstasy stayed still and silent. Tears flooded her face as helicopters hovered from the sky.

Grandma Helen opened her eyes. "It's time for me to go, sweetie. You must go on your own. Don't worry about me," said Grandma Helen.

LAST CHAPTER

"Hands behind your back," Roberts yelled handcuffing Ecstasy.

"Get your hands off my grandmother, don't touch her," she yelled.

The Lieutenant signaled for his team to search the rest of the rooms.

Officers raided Grandma Helen's room recovering The Midnight murder weapons and the masks and hoodies. "We got something!"

Officers raided Ecstasy's room. "We got a dead one in here," the officer announced. Bagz's dead body was covered in blood.

"You're going to jail for the rest of your life. What would make you do something like this?" said Detective Roberts.

"No, no, my grandmom didn't mean to do it, please forgive her, she didn't mean to do it. Grandma! Grandma!" She screamed and kicked. "Granma, why did you do this?!"

"I love you, Ecstasy. You're going to be fine," said Grandma Helen.

The arresting officer had had enough. "Who are you talking to?" He looked around and saw no one.

"My grandmother Helen," Ecstasy replied.

"Your grandmother?" The officer laughed.

"Yes, I love her, please don't take her away," Ecstasy begged.

Carves glanced around the room, along with his fellow officers. "Ma'am, are you taking any medicated drugs of some sort?"

"What is that supposed to mean?"

"It means there's no one here but you. Are you the Midnight Slasher?"

Ecstasy started grinning in such an evil way.

"You must have been talking to a ghost this whole time. Let's take her to the station and book her, we have more than enough evidence."

Officers escorted Ecstasy down a flight of stairs as she screamed, "Grandma!" she cried as they shoved and dragged her to the front door, "Grandma answer me!" she kicked and bit officers.

Outside, the neighbors watched in awe. "Don't make me tase you!" said the officer, pushing her into the back seat of the patrol car.

Back Inside

"Check this out," said Carves to one of the officers.

The detective walked into Grandma Helen's bedroom. A black voodoo doll sat on her old rocking chair.

"I guess this is the grandmother she was referring to," he said pointing at a picture of Grandma Helen.

◆ ◆ ◆

Ecstasy sat in the dim-lit interrogation room, her mind racing a mile a minute. Everything from her childhood to this moment hit like a blade to the gut. The cold metal cuffs on her wrists didn't help. Detective Roberts and Detective Brown exchanged looks before sliding into their seats. Years of bodies turning up dead. Blood on the walls. Now, they had someone to pin it on. Finally, they could close the book on the unsolved murder of Kareem Thomas, Don Franklin, his wife Rianna, and Bagz, who she was found lying next to, dead in the bed. Roberts leaned in; his fingers laced together.

"Ecstasy, we need to know the truth. Why did you kill all these people?" He spread out the crime scene photos in front of her. Every victim stabbed or shot. Blood written on the walls.

She inhaled deep, her eyes glowing with rage. She picked up the picture of Rev Don, her fingers clenching tight. "This son of a bitch killed my grandmother," she muttered, her voice thick with venom. "Nobody did nothing about it!" Her eyes darted to the corner of the room. She saw her grandmother standing there. Sweat trickled down her temple. "Grandmom?" Grandma Helen smiled; her voice soft but strong.

"Don't worry about a damn thing, baby. You gone be just fine."

Brown adjusted his tie, pulling out an old case file. "You were talking to ghosts when we arrested you, huh?" He smirked, tapping the folder. "We know you was tied to Don and Kareem. I got a whole list. Tell us what happened."

Ecstasy's eyes darkened, staring at the table.

"Tell them the truth, baby," Grandma Helen whispered then vanished into thin air. "He was my grandmother secret," Ecstasy said, voice steady but cold. "A man of God in public, but behind closed doors? He had sins of his own." She leaned back; expression unreadable.

"He bought my grandma that house on 16th Street. But when his jealous wife, Rianna, found out? She came to the house in a rage. They argued. Rianna pushed my grandmother down the stairs." Ecstasy's nostrils flared. "She died. And yawl let them go free."

Brown flipped through the file, nodding. "Rianna and Don were questioned back then, but we could never pin nothing on them. It was ruled an accident."

Ecstasy snapped. "Accident my ass. That bastard let her die and kept lying, playing the devoted husband."

Roberts tilted his head, voice firm. "And that's why you killed them?"

Ecstasy's jaw tightened. "No. I killed them because they had something to do with Grandmom losing her damn life!" Her voice boomed through the room, shaking with real rage.

Brown's pen tapped against the table. "Take it easy." He watched how quick she switched from soft and sweet to cold-blooded. That sinister smile. That dead-look in her eyes. The veins on her forehead pulsed like they had their own heartbeat.

"When people meet me, they think I'm just some scared little girl." Ecstasy's lips curled into a slow smirk. "I love it when people underestimate me."

Roberts frowned. "Your grandmother passed, Ecstasy. Your grandmother was found dead in that very house you were arrested in." He slid a yellowed piece of paper across the table. "Her obituary. How can you think she still here?"

Ecstasy froze; her breath stopped. "Don't worry about my connection with my grandmother, motherfucker!" She jerked her cuffs. "My wrists hurt! These cuffs are too damn tight!"

Brown slid a folder toward her, flipping it open. Helen Jordan. Deceased. "Your grandmother a figure of your imagination."

Her world tilted. Memories tangled with reality. The voices, the whispers, the comfort she thought she had was all in her head. Grandma Helen had been dead for years. Yet, Ecstasy had lived like she never left.

"No, she was real. She was with me," Mia whispered, voice cracking. Roberts folded his arms.

"Then tell us why you killed Kareem. Tell us about the others."

Ecstasy exhaled slow, her fingers flexing. "Kareem? That weirdo? He ran his mouth to protect his preacher. He was their key witness." She smirked, tilting her head. "If he had just kept his damn mouth shut, he wouldn't have got un-alived." Then she laughed. That same laugh she had the night she did it. "But then I met Bagz." Her smile faded. "I started seeing them in him too. The lies. The betrayal. The pain." Her fingers curled into fists. "It triggered something in me. I couldn't stop."

Silence filled the room. Outside, thunder rumbled. The storm that started years ago was finally reaching its end. Roberts hit STOP on the tape recorder. The interrogation was over.

Ecstasy watched them walk out the room. Her mind drifted to her brother. Would she ever see him again? A single tear rolled down her cheek.

❖ ❖ ❖

The next morning the walls of a lonely cell spoke to Ecstasy. "Let me out of here!" She screamed at the top of her lungs, "I didn't do anything!"

Ecstasy has finally realized that she is in prison.

"Hey!" she screamed again. She kept screaming at the top of her lungs till she heard the irritating shuffling footsteps of a police district guard. She could also hear the jingle of his keys as he got closer.

Mr. Ferguson is an old Jamaican guy about 6-foot 250 pounds. With each step that he took, Ecstasy could hear the vibration of his stumps and footsteps. As he got closer, crumbs from a brownie fell from his long beard.

He brushed his shirt nonchalantly and noticed the stains on it from his lunch. "Dam it." He said, coming to stand in front of Ecstasy Jorden's cell.

"Somebody, help me! I think a mistake has been made. I'm not supposed to be here!"

No one could hear her from her cold lonely cell, of that, she was sure. Mr. Ferguson opened the food slot on her door just as

Ecstasy repeated herself.

He held a clipboard and wrote a checkmark by her name. He was interested in her pretty, seductive, and innocent look. She didn't seem like a killer. She was too damn pretty, he thought to himself, as he daydreamed of her as the Midnight Slasher.

"What day is it?" she asked, her eyes glued to the window of a secured room.

"It's Friday the 13th," chuckled Mr. Ferguson.

"Oh my god, how long have I been here?"

"I see that your medication is wearing off. You have come to your senses."

Ecstasy remembered passing out at the precinct. She remembered screaming, kicking, and yelling, "I'm innocent." But nobody had listened to her, they wrestled her to the ground, handcuffed her, and kick her in the back.
"I thought I was in a dream." She stared at her room. Her shoes were lying by the steel bench.

Mr. Ferguson rubbed his beard. "I just don't get it."

"Get what, Mr. Ferguson?" She said, reading his name tag.

"How can a sweet, pretty innocent girl like you be such…" he paused. "Brutal killing machine?"

"And what makes you think that I'm a killer? Someone set me up!"

"You were charged with multiple homicides. You are the Midnight Slasher, the serial killer. Who would have known that it would be a woman? I watched the news and saw how you butchered those people and wrote bloody signatures on the wall.

How could you?"

"Before you continue, Mr. Ferguson, understand that I'm innocent of whatever that sheet in your hand says about me, sir. I'm innocent of this one big mistake, please."

She busted into tears. Mr. Ferguson walked away, shaking his head.

"Another day on the job." He could hear Ecstasy crying, "Nooooo!" in her cold cell as he walked away.

TO BE CONTINUED...............

This story was written while I was doing federal time. I wanted to do something different — a murder mystery with a voodoo twist. A lot of us players overlook the real danger that can come with laying down with just anybody. We "wham, bam, thank you ma'am" women without even thinking... but what if one of them wasn't like the rest? What if one out the bunch was insane? A sociopath? Mentally unstable? Or even into dark spiritual work — witchcraft? I've met all kinds of women — victims of their environment, beautiful and broken, beat-down and dangerous. You never know what kind of darkness a woman been through, or what she might do when she's triggered. Truth is, I've had to escape more than one woman's house after I moved in, used the situation for what I could, and dipped when things got too deep.

This ain't just a story. It's a lesson. Be mindful of who you lie down with. Try not to hurt each other out here. Because one day... you might meet a Ecstasy. Peace.

About Author

Umar Quadeer is an influential voice in the urban fiction and street lit genres. His journey began with a signing by national bestselling author Wahida Clark, leading to the release of his debut novel, Enemy Bloodline. Following this successful introduction, Quadeer self-published the captivating series Her Hidden Secrets, and Another Hidden Secret further solidifying his reputation for delivering raw and authentic stories. His latest book, Behind the Trigger, delves deeper into the gritty realities of urban life, showcasing his talent for creating compelling narratives and complex characters. With each new release, Quadeer continues to leave an indelible mark on the urban fiction landscape. In addition to his urban fiction works, Quadeer has ventured into the realm of science fiction with his books UFO in the Bible & Quran, and Gangster Gods.

Follow me on Instagram   umar_quadeer215 YOUTUBE @Trap_pages FACEBOOK UMAR QUADEER TIkTOK Umar Quadeer

Made in the USA
Columbia, SC
30 April 2025